Shielka
Last of the Seers
(Book 1)

Other books by Rory Briski

RUNES

RUNES for: Divination (Basic)
Runes: the ancient and mysterious symbols of a forgotten age.
ISBN: 978-0-9827921-0-0

RUNES for: Divination (Advanced)
ISBN: 978-0-9827921-1-7

AEROSPACE

In-Flight Entertainment & Connectivity
The history and current state of IFEC in Commercial Aircraft and Executive Jets.
ISBN: 978-0-9827921-3-1

PUBLISHING

How To Successfully Self-Publish Your Book For Less Than $20.00
13 simple and cost effective steps to successful self-publishing.
ISBN: 978-0-9827921-2-4

Shielka
Last of the Seers
(Book 1)

By

Rory Briski

DEDICATION

This book is dedicated to my wife Astara, without whom, none of this would have been possible.

DISCLAIMER

All characters appearing in this book are fictitious. Any resemblance to real persons, living or dead, is purely coincidental.

TABLE OF CONTENTS

CHAPTER 1: THE SEERS

The tropical summer sun was unusually hot this year and the heavy rains that typically cascaded down from the sky were strangely absent. Replacing the rain was a thick humidity that sapped the strength and drained the spirit. Stout and hearty palm trees normally accustomed to the tropical summer heat began to wither and die, such was the peculiar nature of the weather this season.

The Isle of the Ikano was one of several small islands that stretched out across the waves. This small island chain was split into two groups. They were laid out so that each island had a twin or sister island just at the horizon.

The tribes that lived on the southern islands were aggressive and constantly looked for war. The most frequent cause of wars between the islands was over fishing rights in the common waters between the two strings of islands. They would seek to cut each others nets and sink their rivals fishing boats. Depending on which side was stronger several things could happen. Occasionally the result would be the payment of several children to the attackers village to bribe them into not attacking again. Another possibility would be payment to the defenders village if the aggressor was too weak to follow up its hostile actions with a full scale war. Typically though there would be an all out war between the two islands until one was clearly victorious.

Historically the winner did not claim the losers' island for their own. Each was content with their own island domain and did not actively seek to conquer the others permanently.

The week had begun on the Isle of the Ikano as usual with little fanfare and much hard work. The neighboring island of the Kanji had declared war on the Ikano village the month before and the fighting trudged along slowly. The constant struggle to make new weapons and care for

1

the dying were taking its toll upon even the hardiest warrior. Of all the members of the village only the Seers were immune to the ravages of war. For none among any tribe would dare risk their wrath. By unwritten law the Seers were a separate entity from the tribe they served. To injure a Seer would bring the fury of all Seers down upon the transgressor, even from the Seers in the offenders own tribe.

Maraka, the most powerful of the Ikano village Seers, had suddenly become very ill. The cause of his illness was a mystery as he had no fever nor scars upon his body. He just lay there asleep, neither eating nor drinking. He was slowly diminishing in size from starvation. Occasionally, he would break out in a cold sweat which gave the healers some hope that his recovery would be soon, but this would never last long and he always returned to his comatose slumber. This condition greatly disturbed the Ikano people because never before in their history had a Seer been ill.

Maraka was old, even the elders within the tribal council remember Maraka as being old and telling them stories when they were small children. Not one person among them could remember a time when Maraka was not present. Maraka now lay still in a death like sleep, he was a trusted advisor and powerful Seer, as such he advocated the use of mind power and not bodily strength. Some of the ancient songs and ballads told of a fierce warrior named Maraka that fought for the Ikano centuries before. For someone to ask him if he had been related to this ancient hero would be a grave insult if he was not. His presence in the village was taken for granted, he was part of their normal lives and the people respected his solitude.

Maraka had learned long ago that true power rests in the mind and not in the frail shell of muscle and bone. In his youth he had been a strong and powerful warrior and saw no need to practice the stupid mental exercises his teachers kept pushing upon him.

If attacked he could fight with his hands, none among his people could defeat him.

"Why bother with stupid tricks of the mind when a strong arm and a good spear are all that are needed?", he would ask.

Then came the evil ones. Maraka stabbed with his spear and cut with his knife but they would not die. One creature ripped the flesh from Marakas' bones with one great swipe of its terrible claws. Maraka knew he was going to die when it picked him up and flew into the air carrying him away from his mountain home. A chill passed through Maraka as the wind cut into his wounds. Maraka cried out in agony and the creature let out a gleeful laugh then struck him again. Maraka fell into unconsciousness. When Maraka awoke it was burning hot and an intense light stung and blinded his eyes.

He cried out in a wailing pitiful scream, "Noooooooo!!!"

That was 300 years ago. And now, Maraka lay still again.

Shortly after the Kanji had left the Ikano island for the day, dark storm clouds began moving into the region. The Ikano were joyous for they reasoned that the storm would make the seas unfit for travel and give them a much needed rest. The Ikano Seers were not so happy as this storm was too quick to form. But they kept silent and watched. They probed the storm with their minds to see if they could find anything unusual.

There was something strange, that was certain, but they lacked the knowledge to understand what it was.

Some of the Ikano Seers had troubled dreams filled with terrible visions of demons and flames. As the Seers talked of these dreams they began to wonder if there was a connection between Marakas' illness and these night-

3

mares. In these dreams some saw Maraka fighting the Demons in a great void filled with fire and ice.

The Kanji were a mighty foe and had frequently battled the Ikano. But never before had they fought with such intensity and bloodlust. A common thought began to emerge among the Ikano Seers that this war was brought upon them not by the Kanji, but by some greater supernatural force. The dreams now made sense. Maraka was not ill, but had caused his spirit to leave his body. In this way he could do battle with the demons that possessed the Kanji, unhampered by the physical limitations of flesh and blood.

Few among the Seers had mastered the ability to project the mind and detach it from the body. It was a dangerous task as the only link while separated was a thin silvery cord that extended through the nothingness from mind to body. More then one Seer had carelessly caused this cord to be broken while traveling on another plane. It was not a task to be done lightly.

Maraka was the guardian of a young Seer named Shielka. Shielka had shown the promise of great abilities and when fully trained would be a powerful Seer. Her parents were killed years earlier in another battle with the Kanji. Maraka took care of her after she first displayed signs of having the power. He had never seen the power manifest itself so strongly in someone without training. It was important that she receive the strictest instruction and guidance in its proper use. More then one Seer had been lured by others to use the power for personal gain and wealth. When that happened it took the combined might of several Seers to destroy the traitor. If Shielka ever strayed toward evil he wondered if even the combined might of all the other Seers could resist her. Such was the depth of her power.

In any village there were only a handful of Seers. They were the ones who called the fish into the nets, if rain was needed then they called the clouds. They helped crops grow and assisted the healers in curing some minor injuries. Even though they had great energies at their command with which a few short words could level a small mountain, by common agreement they did not use these energies to war against each other.

But they did train for war. Offense and defense, day and night they trained. No one could ever be one hundred percent sure that another village would not convince their Seers to use these awesome powers against them. So they practiced just in case. It was during these practice sessions that Maraka worried the most. For it was during one of these times that he saw the destructive potential of Shielka's talent fully unleashed.

It was Shielka's first failure.

CHAPTER 2: BETRAYED

The night was dark and moonless, the heavy storm clouds that had been approaching now blanketed the sky directly over the Ikano Island. The air was very heavy and difficult to breath.

Shielka slowly sat up in bed and called out, "Who's there?" She was sure that she had heard someone call her name. She sat up and listened but the voice was gone.

"Strange," she thought.

She was sure she had heard something. Then as she laid her head back down upon the feather pillow she felt it, the familiar tingling sensation of the touch of Marakas' mind against hers. He was telling her, no, commanding her to leave immediately. "Take little and leave tonight, most importantly tell no one." Shielka felt afraid and confused.

As tears streamed down her cheeks she asked, "Why?"

His only response was, "We have been betrayed" and then the contact was broken.

She wanted to tell someone and say it was just a dream, but she knew it wasn't. She knew...

She tried to think what she should take but everything was so confused. She finally decided that the less she carried the faster she could go. With that in mind she put some fruit and dried fish into a small pack along with some extra clothing and she was ready. A thought struck her that she should take a weapon of some kind. Without further concern she took a jeweled dagger and a slender staff. These had previously been used by the Seers only for major ceremonies and energy channeling but now they were for survival.

"Where will I go?", she thought, "The far side of the island, the caves that honeycombed through the mountains, the caves will be safe." She held onto that thought, "The Mountain Caves."

As she carefully finished gathering her belongings she wondered about Maraka, "Is he really alright now? His mind had felt so strong and powerful."

She had to find out. She decided that on her way out of the village she would creep into the Healers tent and say good-bye in person. She could not just leave and not speak to him again. After all, he was like a father to her. When Shielka entered the Healers tent she saw that Maraka was still lying on a large bed made of brightly colored feathers, just as he had been during his illness. The soft glow of candlelight made the colors dance and swirl around him.

Shielka quickly moved closer to him but then jumped back. She saw his pale face and still form and reached out with her mind... Nothing. She knew at once he was dead. The grief caused her eyes to moisten but before she could cry she heard strange voices outside the tent. Acting quickly she hid in a corner of the tent behind a large rattan chair. The voices drew nearer, harsh unfamiliar voices, the village had been invaded.

"Too late," she thought, "Too late. I should have listened and left right away."

Then she noticed Marakas' ring. It was pulsating with an eerie green glow that seemed to call to her very soul. Silently and hesitantly she crept out of her hiding place and took the ring from his lifeless finger. Slowly she put it on.

At that very instant the tent flap was ripped apart and Shielka whirled about to see a creature from her worst nightmare standing before her. It towered over her with a red scaly hide and black leathery wings. Its head supported three short horns and its mouth held rows of sharp fangs. The creatures saliva made a hissing sound as it dripped onto the ground. Its claws clicked open and closed

7

as its powerful arms reached for her. Shielka screamed. But even in that split second of terror her Seer training came through. The power that had been locked inside of her came flowing forth. Not by her controlling it by conscious thought, but purely by the reflex action of persistent training. The magnitude of the power was like nothing she had ever felt before. A flash of brilliant white light shot from her forehead and pierced the creatures' skull. The light streamed from Shielka and enveloped the Demon as it fell screaming to the floor. The light flared up for an instant and then the Demon faded into nothingness.

"Flee!", she thought and suddenly she also vanished.

The Kanji invaders and Demons quickly began slaughtering the Ikano people. All was in a state of confusion. What had happened to the guards, and lookouts? In the midst of the chaos the ground started to shake and a loud rumbling could be heard and felt. Then without further warning the mighty volcano that rested in the center of the Ikano island erupted. Both the Kanji and Ikano were surprised. The Demons just laughed and flew away. The first part of their plan had worked flawlessly. The faces of the Kanji warriors went blank the instant the Demons fled and they stood in place dazed. The Elders of both tribes stared up at the billowing fury being unleashed by the mighty volcano.

In amazement they wondered, "Why?"

Then in an enormous primal upheaval the island went up in a ball of flames and sank beneath the raging waves of the ocean.

CHAPTER 3: SAFE ?

Shielka awoke in a cavern filled with strange mystical symbols and the heavy smell of incense. Her mind was confused and her vision went in and out of focus. She was not alone. She was being watched by a fierce looking creature unlike anything she had ever seen. It was covered with long golden hair and had midnight black eyes. Its four muscular legs ended in sharp claws. Long pointed teeth protruded from its snout. The beasts long tail move rhythmically back and forth as it watched her.

She tried to cast a spell to protect herself from the creature but she was too dazed. Shielka kept fading in and out of consciousness and each time that she opened her eyes the creature would be there looking at her. Sometimes a long black tongue would be hanging lazily out of the side of its mouth. After a while and despite its appearance Shielka became accustomed to it and no longer felt threatened. At one point Shielka felt good enough to sit up. However, when she tried it a tremendous pain shot through her head and she collapsed back onto the bed.

Shielka was brought back to consciousness by a heavy weight upon her chest and the feel of something licking her face. As she opened her eyes she saw the beasts head just inches from her own. Instinctively she pushed at it and the creature jumped away from her. Shielka tried to sit up again but a large pair of hands grabbed her shoulders and held her down.

An elderly mans voice said, "Be still, you're hurt."

Turning her head she saw that a man dressed in crimson robes was holding her down.

She lay still and he released her.

"Who are you," he asked, "Where did you come from?"

But she just answered with silence. It took a couple of days before she could move. Even then she had to take care to move very slowly. Once when the man was out she began exploring the cave. Her things were all at the foot of the bed, neatly stacked. Even her dagger and staff were there. The cave was modestly furnished with a bed, table and a couple of chairs. Little else in the cave caught her eye. Except of course the beast. It never left her side. She had gotten over her fear and came to realize that the beast was just as curious about her as she was of it.

When the man returned again, she spoke, "Who are you and where am I? What is this place?"

Unfortunately, the man was carrying in her dinner at the time and was so startled by her sudden speech he jumped, sending the food everywhere. She began laughing immediately, great fits of laughter as if she had never laughed before. The beast was elated and began eating the spilled food furiously as if it was on the verge of starvation. The man just sat where he landed and looked bewildered.

Slowly he to began laughing too and together they laughed until their sides ached. He was the first to recover and quickly returned to his feet.

"Young lady it's not polite to scare the daylights out of your elders."

Upon hearing this she began laughing harder. He frowned and stomped out of the room.

As her strength returned to her she began exploring more and more of her strange new home. The cave she had been in was only a small part of a much larger series of interconnecting caverns and passageways. On her island home she had explored many caves but none like these. What she was in now was clearly not natural. How they were made she did not know, but they were just too perfect to be formed by nature. There were rooms of many shapes and sizes filled with all manner of furnishings and instruments whose purpose she could only guess at.

She had learned that the man's name was Aka'r and that he was apparently alone in this huge place as she saw no one else. Alone except for herself and the beast. The beast he called Ding'ger. Well they weren't entirely alone. There were numerous occasions when a small fuzzy creature would scurry down a path and Ding'ger would chase it. Usually killing it outright. Rarely did one escape Ding'gers notice. Shielka quickly realized what an asset the beast was as a guard. From that time onward Shielka kept a close watch on Ding'ger for signs of danger.

When Shielka was alone she practiced. She practiced with a determination the no Seer before her ever had. The drills that Maraka had taught her as a child to focus her thoughts and energy she now repeated constantly. But all this she did in secret. She told Aka'r that she didn't remember anything. He said she could stay as long as she liked and that maybe he could help her remember. She hated to lie to him but she couldn't be sure she could trust him.

"What does he know of Seers? Of the power they can control? Until I know more about any other people, for there must be others somewhere, I have to maintain my secret."

CHAPTER 4: THE TRUTH REVEALED

One day when Aka'r returned he wasn't alone. Another man in the same type of crimson robes was with him. Aka'r wore a robe with 5 gold bands across the bottom while this other man had three. Shielka wondered about their significance.

"Shielka, this is Fal'r."

Fal'r appeared to be a little younger then Aka'r but not by much.

"Greetings Shielka. Aka'r explained your memory loss to me and asked for my help."

"Fal'r is a great master of the art of telepathy, communicating with the mind. We would like your consent to have Fal'r look into your mind to see who you are and how you came to be in this place."

Shielka began to shake with fear.

"Look into my mind!", she thought, "only a Seer has the ability to do that."

At once she stood up. Her mind was clear as she began the enchantment to protect herself from this mental invasion. Shock shown clearly upon the men's faces when they realized that she was casting a spell. They stood also and cast enchantments upon themselves to protect them from whatever it was that she was doing. But Shielka did nothing except stand there on her guard. Her arms crossed in front of her, close to her chest. Her palms faced outward with her fingers spread.

They stood this way for several moments before Aka'r sat back down. Fal'r sat down also.

"Sit down Shielka," said Aka'r, "We will not attempt to link with your mind if you do not want us to. It isn't necessary anyway as you never lost your memory." Aka'r looked saddened by this revelation. Shielka sat back down but kept her arms up before her.

"Who are you?", Aka'r asked impatiently.

Shielka answered slowly, "My name is as I said before, Shielka."

"Who sent you here and where are you from? Clearly you are not from this region of the world. Your brown skin and snakelike clothing says as much. You're from across the great sea I would imagine."

"Since I don't know where I am I can't say how I got here. No one sent me... I came here by accident.

"Who taught you the magic? What is your masters name?" Fal'r asked.

"I HAVE NO MASTER!" Shielka yelled.

Her anger built up inside her now as thoughts of Maraka and her people dying came to her mind. Energy started to crackle between her fingers as she stared at the two men. They just sat in their chairs watching her.

Aka'r was the next to speak, "In order to control the energy properly, the mind must remain calm. It would be a simple matter now for either Fal'r or myself to break through your mental barriers. Whoever your master is, he or she should have taught you to remain relaxed in stressful situations. If you do not, then terrible accidents can happen. And if truly you have no master, than it's a wonder you are even alive."

The energy she was releasing stopped. She didn't know what to do. She then lowered her hands and looked at Aka'r, her eyes pleading. Ara'r then said, "You have nothing to fear here child tell us what happened."

13

Then it seemed as if a great weight was lifted from her shoulders. She began telling them of her life on the island as an Ikano Seer, of her village and the terrible war of demons. Finally she told of Maraka's death and the destruction of her people.

Aka'r and Fal'r were silent for a long time afterward.

Finally Fal'r said, "but how did you escape?"

"I don't know, I just thought to flee to the mountain caves and that's the last thing that I remember."

"There are no islands in this land as we are very far from the sea. Your story is fantastic and if I were less knowledgeable about the mystic arts I would surely not believe such a tale. But I do believe you."

Aka'r agreed, "it is difficult to believe such a story, but I believe it also. You said that you were fleeing from a great evil. Well, there is surely no safer place in all the world then here in Cloud Mountain. But listen carefully Shielka, in order to be transported such a great distance and to penetrate our protective barriers took an immense amount of power. You must be very careful. We can teach you how to control your magic, but in return we would like you to teach us its source."

Shielka was silent this time. She had not expected this response, but she agreed partly. "If you will consent to the Test of the Seer, and if you pass, then I will teach you what I know. In return, I will accept your offer to teach me your ways and source of power as well."

CHAPTER 5: THE CHOICE

Aka'r and Fal'r had been gone for some time when Shielka finally got up and went back to her room.

"The Test of the Seer" she said softly.

It had been such a long time ago and yet she remembered it so well.

"But can I administer the test when I'm not in complete control of the power myself? These men are masters of their craft. Magic they called it. A name for the power they used."

The Seers of her people just called it Power. For that is what it was, energy. Like the lightning on a stormy day but infinitely more powerful. For it encompassed everything. Everything that lived and everything that didn't. When channeling the power it was like riding on the waves of the ocean. The power ebbed and flowed but always remained immensely strong and dangerous.

"I must know more about these men before I can release such energy among them."

With that thought she felt a tingling sensation within her being that seemed to reaffirm that her choice had been a good one. Then as suddenly as the sensation had come, it vanished. The feeling was eerie. It made her skin crawl as if someone or something had read her thoughts. She carefully checked each of the mental barriers that protected her psyche and all were intact.

"Just nerves", she thought, "just nerves."

"I have to know more about this place, but how? I can't just go out and explore it... Or can I?"

That night she prepared for the separation. She received much training from Maraka and had studied ev-

15

erything he said with great intensity. But he had only just begun teaching her the ways of separating the mind and body. If she could not master it on the first try there would be no second chance.

She meditated in silence for several long hours before finally willing her mind to go forth. She saw herself then, sitting in the lotus position, arms outstretched upon her knees. It was a strange wonderful feeling, as if floating in the water on a hot summer day. Then she saw it and was afraid. The thin silver cord that connected her mind and body, such a fragile looking thing. It was like a long strand of a spiders web, glistening as if wet with a mornings dew. She had willed that her dagger and staff be projected with her and she checked to see if they had been. All was well, her dagger was safely sheathed at the top of her thigh and she had the staff in hand.

Now it was time to get moving. To investigate this place and its people. As she looked around the room she noticed a rainbow pattern around the door. The energy of a spell. Not wanting to take the chance of disturbing the barrier she simply walked through the wall.

This wall was part of a long hallway. She had suspected its existence. Quickly she glanced around at the Silver Cord, it was still there, a good sign anyway. She decided to travel toward the center of the mountain. This is where they would have their most sacred and secret knowledge. In that place she could determine their true nature.

She started to glide down the passageway, slowly at first then gaining speed as she went. She passed several people along her journey, all were oblivious to her passage. After a while the passageways became empty and desolate. As she rounded one of the many corners she saw a huge creature, and she knew it saw her as well. This was a hideous creature chained in front of a huge door by a single golden thread. It was nearly twice her height with leath-

16

ery moss green skin and long spindly arms that ended in sharp claws. It howled as it saw her and lunged forward. She ducked as it reached for her and only the momentum she had picked up in travel allowed her to pass by the creature.

It screamed as she shot past it, and it turned to watch as she flew through the door.

On this side of the door she was enveloped in darkness. She willed herself to stop moving and abruptly she did so. Her mind recoiled from the terror she just narrowly escaped. Suddenly she felt herself being pulled toward the door. Being pulled by her silver cord! The creature must have grabbed it like a rope and was now pulling her back through the door.

CHAPTER 6: THE WARNING

Aka'r was not sleeping very well. He tossed and turned as his dreams were full of demons and devils. So vivid were his dreams that he abruptly awoke covered with sweat.

"A warning", he said. "I have not dreamed of the Dark Ones for over 300 years."

Three hundred years ago the hosts of evil walked boldly upon the land. In great numbers they had come across the void to enslave his world. Only after many great battles were fought did he and his people defeat the creatures of darkness and restore order their kingdom. Some of his closest friends were killed in these battles. Men and women of great power and courage. There are now less then a quarter the number of Master Mage's around than during that time.

There was a knock upon his door. He sensed the presence of Fal'r and let him into his room.

"Fal'r, what brings you here this late at night?"

"Dreams. Dreams filled with demons. I have been thinking of what Shielka had said. If what she said was true, then the demons have returned. This time however, they chose to take on a less populated part of the world. A foothold is all they need. From this isolated area they can build and expand with none of us aware of what they are doing until its too late."

"So it is now confirmed, a dream warning has been received. The intensity of the dreams and their clear focus would indicate that they were deliberately sent, not randomly picked up as dreams usually are."

Aka'r was up and dressed now pacing back and forth across his room.

"Who could have sent us that warning? What power

did we now face that could penetrate the magical barriers around our citadel with impunity. Shielka had done it also. We must speak with her."

So off they went toward Shielka's room. Ding'ger was with them. Aka'r's constant pacing had awakened the creature. As they neared Shielka's room Ding'ger began making a high pitched whining sound and bolted forward toward her door.

"Ding'ger stop!"

But Ding'ger paid no attention and crashed into the door. Normally his weight and great strength would have shattered the door. Unfortunately due to the enchantments Aka'r had placed upon the door, the door held and Ding'ger was knocked to the ground dazed. Aka'r and Fal'r ran to where the beast lay. Fal'r checked Ding'ger to see if she was still alive.

"There doesn't seem to be any permanent damage."

"What had gotten into her?"

Aka'r checked the integrity of the spell he had cast on Shielka's door.

"The enchantments on the door are still intact. She's still inside."

He knocked on the door. He was answered by a deathly silence. Clearing the enchantments he opened the door and saw Shielka sitting up in bed with her eyes closed. She was very pale. He moved closer to her and noticed that she didn't appear to be breathing.

"DEAD?" he yelled.

Fal'r immediately sent his mind forth to see if any remnant of life was still within her.

His mind slammed against the barriers that Shielka had erected to protect the shell of her body from possession. He screamed in agony and his body dropped to the ground unconscious.

Aka'r put up protective barriers around himself and braced for Shielka's mental attack, but none came.

Ding'ger was awake now and moved to where Fal'r had collapsed. He sniffed a few times and then moved to where Shielka was. Ding'ger cocked his head to one side and whined. Aka'r was confused by the events of the past few minutes. He finally decided that whatever had happened it was over and he had better tend to Fal'r.

Fal'r was unconscious and his breathing was shallow. Except for the minor cuts and scrapes he received when impacting the floor, nothing physical was wrong. It was now Aka'r's turn to send out his mind. He cautiously touched the fringes of Fal'r's essence and met no resistance. Fal'r's mind had been stunned. No permanent damage had been done, his aura was still intact.

Carefully Aka'r began to clear away the fog that clouded his friends thoughts. With painstaking care Aka'r cleared layer after layer of mist until finally Fal'r responded. Slowly at first then with greater strength his mind pushed through to meet Aka'r. Their minds had merged to transfer information in this manner hundreds of times in the past. So Fal'r easily recognized Aka'r's presence and allowed the merge to take place.

Aka'r then realized what had happened to Fal'r. Shielka had erected barriers around herself to prevent anyone or anything from intruding upon her mind.

As Aka'r withdrew from Fal'r's mind, Aka'r's minds eye caught the slightest glimmer of silver around Shielka.

"What was that?", Aka'r said rather puzzled.

20

He then cast a spell which allowed him to look into the astral plane.

"No!"

Now he could finally comprehend what she had done.

CHAPTER 7: THE GUARDIAN OF KORTAN

"AIEEEEEEEEEEEEEEEEEEE", she screamed.

But no one was there to hear her. She tried to will herself to stop but to no avail. She could not compete with the monsters great strength. In another few precious moments she would be pulled through the door, into the grasp of that horrifying creature. Then she felt the vibrations of the blast. Someone had triggered the defenses she had put around her physical self. She was about to die, either by this monster or by the forces that threatened to destroy her body.

She had nothing to lose. She had risked everything in an effort to discover the secret of this mountain and had now lost. But she would not die alone. She quickly calmed her mind and drew in the powerful forces of nature.

" Shielka..." she felt a distant voice say.

"Shielka wait. Use the Staff of Oralin against the creature. The Staff of Oralin", the voice said.

"Maraka!" Shielka cried out as she recognized Maraka's voice.

But contact was broken, and she was alone again. Then as she had done all of her life she immediately carried out her mentors orders. She willed the slender staff she carried to life. She poured wave upon wave of energy into it until the staff glowed with raw power. She then calmly allowed herself to be pulled through the door and faced the creature.

The monster dropped Shielka's silver cord, threw out its clawed hands and lunged for her throat. Shielka quickly brought the staff up and struck one of the creatures arms. Energy erupted along the creatures arm and showers of sparks flew from the impact.

The monster was thrown back and it slammed into the rocky wall behind it.

Since the time it was first put into service here to guard this chamber, many have tried to get past it. All have failed. Never before had one of these puny human intruders caused it pain. It was a Guardian of Kortan. One of the most powerful creatures in the universe. Its usefulness as a guardian comes from its great strength, high intellect and keen sight. Its vision was such that it could see into other dimensions and planes of existence. Its only known weakness was one of greed. For a price it would guard a treasure for 500 years. But at the end of that time it could claim the treasure for its own. Some have foolishly tried to kill the creature and keep the treasure for themselves but none have ever succeeded.

Shielka was the first one to have ever caused it pain and it was furious. However, it did not immediately launch a counter attack.

It quickly formulated its plan and then spoke in a deep guttural voice, "Who are you?."

Shielka was poised for another strike, energy poured into her staff. She was taken aback by the creatures question. This was something that she had not expected.

"I am Shielka, Seer of the Ikano", she replied, "Who are you?"

The guttural voice responded, "I am Kondore - a Guardian of Kortan."

Shielka guessed that by the way he responded that being a Guardian of Kortan must have some significance but she had no idea what it might be.

"This area is forbidden to all."

"What is it that you guard here?"

"I guard that which I have been given to guard, none may pass by me."

Shielka stayed poised at the ready awaiting a surprise attack from Kondore. Her muscles grew tense as she waited.

"Return from whence you came human", Kondore's deep voice seemed to grow and it filled the cave with an empty hollow sound.

Shielka thought about what Kondore had said, "None may enter and forbidden to all."

She spoke a bit more slowly and distinctly this time, "You said none may enter, what about he who commands you?"

"He who set me here to guard has been dead nearly 300 years. He no longer lives. No one may pass."

"What of Aka'r?"

"You speak of the crimson fool. He has tried many times to pass. But it is forbidden."

Kondore began shifting about, eager for battle but waiting a little longer to strike. This cat and mouse game was one he had not had the pleasure of enjoying for a long long time. He would regret killing this one, she showed spirit and intelligence.

"You guard but no one commands. How long must you guard before being set free?"

Kondore spoke with a laugh, "In 150 years time I will be free of my bondage, then power and glory will be mine for eternity."

"If your master is dead who will set you free? And what power will you possess? What is it that you guard here?"

Kondore had enough of this game, it was time to end it. But he would answer this last question, for it would be fun to watch the humans response to his answer.

Kondore then sat down upon his heels and rested his weight upon the balls of his feet. To Shielka it seemed as though he was surrendering as she saw no means that he could attack. Actually, this was a prime position for Kondore as he would be able to spring up and leap upon his opponent with great speed.

Kondore then spoke in a more friendly manner, "After 500 years of service, the golden cord will dissolve. I will be set free. In a short time I will be in possession of 'The ORB of Orion.' "

Kondore watched for Shielka's face to be engulfed in terror but she just looked at him blankly.

Shielka observed that after speaking Kondore got a very strange look upon his face. He almost looked comically puzzled.

Shielka responded, "So?"

Kondore was indeed surprised, he had credited this human with above average intelligence, but now to discover she doesn't know of 'The ORB of Orion'? This was just too much to take. Kondore suddenly spun about and turned his head and looked down the hall. Shielka fearing an attack from where Kondore was looking swung around and faced down the long hall as well. In that instant, Kondore sprung sideways from his crouching position with great speed and agility. Leaping up in a fluid cat like motion he crashed down upon Shielka smashing her into the cold stone floor beneath them.

CHAPTER 8: THE TARGET

Aka'r tended to Fal'r while he tried to decide on a course of action.

"Astral Projection", Aka'r said aloud, "if I had only known she was capable."

Aka'r began to wonder if Shielka's condition had been just a clever trap.

"She's after the Orb. She has to be stopped," he yelled.

Fal'r was regaining consciousness so Aka'r decided that it was critical to stop Shielka before she released Kondore and gained possession of the Orb. Aka'r gave Ding'ger the command to protect Fal'r and then readied himself. Aka'r was a master of his craft and it was an easy matter for him to cast the necessary spell to travel into the astral plane.

Aka'r quickly stepped through the wall and began following Shielka's path. It was not as direct as he thought it would be.

"She must not have studied our caves before venturing forth", he thought, "very poor planning for a thief."

The further he traveled the madder he became. By the time he reached the last turn to the 'Chamber of the Orb' he was furious.

Not knowing what to expect when he rounded the corner he put up his psychic defenses and readied some very powerful offensive spells. Carefully he peered around the edge of the wall. He was not surprised to see Shielka speaking with Kondore. Kondore was relaxing, sitting on his haunches, Shielka looked casual.

"I must do something before they strike up an alliance", he thought.

If Aka'r had been thinking clearly he would have re-membered the story about 'The Guardian of Kortan' and not worried about any type of alliance. But such was not the case. Aka'r stepped out from behind the wall into the center of the hallway. Kondore's keen hearing picked up Aka'r's footsteps and Kondore wheeled about to face Aka'r. Then when Shielka turned as well, Kondore saw his chance.

"This is working out better then I expected", Kondore thought.

Then Kondore leaped sideways upon the unsuspecting Shielka. Unfortunately, at that same instant in time Aka'r released a massive burst of energy in the form of a Light-ning Bolt. This bolt struck Kondore fully and slammed him sideways knocking him clear of Shielka. Shielka was hit with an immense amount of energy as well. She lay still on the ground, her clothes smoldering.

Kondore raised himself up off of the ground and turned to face Aka'r.

"You have spoiled my fun. I don't like to eat fried hu-mans."

Kondore did not think Aka'r would attack him with spells while he was fighting the girl.

"These humans are so unpredictable", Kondore thought, "the world would be better without them."

Kondore was ready now. The Lightning Bolt had in-jured him slightly because he wasn't prepared for it. But now Aka'r would have to come in closer to do battle with short range spells. The long range spells have little effect on a 'Guardian' when they are prepared for them. Aka'r planned his strategy and moved in closer.

"It is too bad about having to kill Shielka", Aka'r thought, "but she was a thief and I had to keep her away from the Orb at all costs."

Then Aka'r and Kondore closed upon one another. Spell, claw, parry, counter spell, it went on and on. Aka'r had more stamina then it appeared for his advanced age and handled himself quite well in combat. Kondore was also a seasoned warrior with thousands of victories to his credit. As these two battled they did not notice the still form of Shielka on the ground begin to move.

She moved very slowly, only a finger at first and then an arm. Then the other arm, soon she was crawling ever so slowly across the floor toward the forbidden door.

When she had made it through she began going over the last few minutes of her life. She was alive because she was channeling energy into the staff when the Lightning Bolt struck. Her staff absorbed most of the energy intended for her. It now lay fully charged but out in the other hallway. Shielka reflected on the monsters immense weight crushing down on her, it was horrible. Shielka had long gashes in her arms where the monster had clawed at her.

"I am alive for now, but for how much longer?", she wondered.

With the small amount of strength she had left she drew her slender dagger. Upon drawing it from its sheath it began to glow, faintly at first and then brighter and brighter. She looked around this cavern and caught a glimpse of what the fight must be all about. There, in the center of the room, was a raised pedestal in the shape of a huge reptile claw. Between the three talons was a six inch Pearl sphere, with gold and platinum bands around it.

The sphere seemed to call to her, to beg her to pick it up. She tried to step back but the call was overpowering.

"I have to have it", she thought.

Without thinking she reached out and plucked it from its resting place.

As soon as it was free of the talons the pedestal crumbled to the ground and turned to dust. Immediately the ground started to shake. Aka'r and Kondore stopped in their struggles and looked at each other in shock. Kondore noticed Shielka was missing and screamed, as he realized what had happened. He had lost to a lowly human girl, and then he faded into nothingness, cast out of this world back to his own plane of existence for a thousand years.

Aka'r was hysterical as he moved forward dodging pieces of falling ceiling. He stepped though the door to see Shielka beginning to fade as well.

"Stop!", he commanded.

Shielka turned to face him, a strange penetrating expression on her face. Aka'r believed this look was one of madness and he readied himself for an even greater battle then that with Kondore.

But Shielka just smiled and faded away.

CHAPTER 9: THE ORB OF ORION

Shielka was floating now, carried along on the Astral Winds. With every beat of her heart she felt the power of the Orb pumping into her veins. Power, the pure energy of life. The Orb was channeling this energy into Shielka's body at an ever increasing rate. Her entire essence began to pulse to the beat of the Orb. Slowly at first and then gradually it quickened its pace to beat faster and faster. Shielka was being consumed by the power of the Orb.

At the height of her euphoria a severe burning sensation shot into her hand. The pain was excruciating and it quickly spread from her finger, to her hand, to her arm, chest and body. A hot blazing fire that knotted her stomach and seared its way into her mind.

"Shielka!" the fire bellowed, "Shielka!, control the Orb, control the Power or die!"

"The pain!", Shielka screamed, "Stop the Pain!"

Slowly a small part of her mind began to rebel against this torture. It began to reject the influx of power and fire, it pushed against this onslaught of energy with barriers of her own. After an agonizingly long period time her own energy field, coupled with the power the Orb had supplied her with, erected a strong enough barrier to stop all magic from passing through it. Shielka could think clearly again.

With puzzled amazement she looked down at the blackened band around her finger. The burning sensation had come from Maraka's ring. Maraka had saved her again. At last she understood, Maraka saw what was going to happen to their island home and there was no way that he could prevent it. He had cast a spell that enabled his life force to be transferred from his body into the gemstone of his ring. He had been with her the entire time, helping and guiding her as best he could.

The Orb had almost stolen her mind and spirit, its power was great and she would have to be very careful when calling upon its energies.

***

Aka'r slowly picked himself up from where he sat. The tremors of the earthquake had stopped.

"It's over," he thought, if the Demons have really returned then the Orb would have helped even the odds in my peoples' favor. But now?"

He glided back toward where he had left Fal'r and Ding'ger. He felt very tired and worn, the battle with Kondore had weakened him more then he allowed himself to believe.

When Aka'r reached Shielka's room Fal'r was sitting propped up against the wall, with Ding'ger whining at his feet. Shielka's body was gone. He quickly checked over Fal'r to see if there was any serious damage that he had not noted earlier, but found none. Aka'r slowly told him of the events that happened since Fal'r fell unconscious. Fal'r turned pale as Aka'r told of Shielka obtaining the Orb.

They both sat in silence for a long time.

***

Shielka found herself in a beautiful green valley serenely tucked away between two mountain ranges. The Orb was safely tucked away in a pouch at her side. The bright yellow sun cast warm radiant heat down across her shoulders and face. After spending so much time inside the mountain it was good to be outside again.

She sat down upon a small outcropping of rock and stared at the green ring upon her finger. Slowly she sent her mind forth into the ring. She felt the protective barriers that Maraka had erected to guard his psyche.

As the barriers were slowly lowered she felt at peace again. Marakas' mind felt strong and full of vigor. She transferred the details of what had happened into his mind hastily but careful not to leave out any of the details. For while Maraka had been with her the entire time, to see beyond the gemstone took great amounts of energy and severely taxed his strength.

"What is the power of the Orb and where did it come from?", Shielka asked Maraka.

Maraka responded, "The Orb of Orion is as old as the very ground you now walk upon. It is said that when the Gods first contemplated creating the heavens and earth that they made three Orbs to help them in their task. The first was the Orb of Caecum, ever called The Sculptor's Tool. For this was the Orb that fashioned the mountains and the lands. The second Orb was The Orb of Aquarius, the symbol of The Water Bearer. The oceans, lakes, streams and rivers were created by the power of this Orb. As you may guess these two Orbs are opposed to one another and their powers constantly fight to shape and reshape the surface of the earth. With the creation of the planet the Gods began to populate it with various types of living creatures, plants and animals. To more easily control the creatures they had made, the Gods fashioned the Orb of Orion, The Giant Hunter. In this Orb, they instilled the Magic to give and take the energy of life and power. To bend it to the will of its possessor. The intent was to use the energy gained to create an immense creature or giant out of pure energy. In this way the Gods could maintain order without their direct personal intervention and use of their stored energy reserves.

The Orb of Orion was handed down from generation to generation from King to King for thousands of years. The only time it had ever been used was during the Time of the Awakening.

In ages past an evil Seer, or Sorceress as people here call them, cast mighty enchantments upon a huge statue that had been fashioned from thousands of gemstones. These gems had been fused together in such a way as to create one massive multicolored entity of enormous size. The power of this Seer was so great that she gave this entity a life of its own. But with that life she unwittingly gave it power. For in her haste to create this massive being she failed to notice the manipulations of a demon that had crept upon this world unnoticed. Then while she cast the final enchantments upon the gemstones, the Demon entered the gems and was itself fused into the power grid of the crystalline structure. She had planned to use this creature to enslave the world but she herself became a slave to its awesome demonic strength.

The creatures power grew with every mind it consumed, its strength was increasing at an incredible rate. When King Cepheus, the keeper of the Orb of Orion, finally heard of what was happening he feared that he couldn't control the power of the Orb alone. With that fear in place he called together all of the Wizards of the land, regardless of their power or ability, and commanded them thusly, 'You must create a spell that when cast into the Orb will combine all of your energies to form The Giant Hunter to combat this Demon and banish it from our lives forever.'

The Wizards gathered together and worked day and night for seven days before returning to the King. The King brought the Orb out of its hiding place and set it upon a pedestal that was in the shape of a three fingered dragons claw. The Wizards gathered around it and began casting their spell. At first nothing happened, but then slowly the Orb began to spin within the claw. Faster and faster it spun until the golden bands that surrounded it were nothing but a blur. Energy poured forth from the Wizards minds and many of the lesser magic users dropped from the fatigue. Eventually a great form began to take shape above the Orb.

A huge Titan of a man with long black hair and cold grey eyes. He instinctively knew his purpose and in two strides of his long muscular legs he was through the wall and walking toward the domain of the Gemstone Demon.

The Demon was not without power of its own and sensed the approach of the Titan. The Demon tried casting enchantments upon the Titan but all the magic attacks served to do was strengthen the Titan, and the Demon quickly ceased this method of attack. The Demon then called forth a host of its Demon-kind and sent them out to destroy the humans that fashioned this Titan. A battle then began within the Kingdom of Cepheus against a hoard of Demons, red as fire and cold as a winter snow. The Kings guards fought with all their might and some of the Wizards that were pouring energy into the Orb were called out to assist in the battle against the Demon host. The battle was not going well for the humans.

Elsewhere the Titan advanced close enough to engage the Demon directly and did so with spells of its own. But the Demon was immune to the effects of spells as its form was naught but a vast chamber of energy. The fighting quickly turned to hand-to-hand. The powers that were unleashed were awesome. The ground shook for hundreds of miles in all directions with the fierceness of an earthquake.

As the two creatures continued to battle, more and more of the Wizards fell exhausted to the ground. Something had to give and give soon or all would be lost. Seeing the fate of the world begin to slip, King Cepheus called upon the Orb with enchantments of his own. He called forth and awakened the Sleeping God of Fornax.

Within the depths of the realm of Fornax there was forged the mighty Sword of Orion. It had remained unused since the beginning of time and now was the hour to draw it forth. But in awakening Fornax there was a great upheaval of land and a great mountain was created that reached into the very clouds. This was the creation of Cloud Mountain.

Fornax was enraged at the mortal King for disturbing his slumber, but noting the battle that raged between the Titan and the Demon, Fornax consented to hear the Kings request. As the Orb of Orion was used to create the Titan that battled for the good of the world, it was fitting the he be allowed to wield the Sword of Orion against this demonic creature. In return for the use of the sword the King proposed that a full one half of his kingdom would go with Fornax and work in his great foundry below the earth.

Fornax laughed and said, "All or Nothing, I care little for this world my brethren created but help with the smelter and forge would be useful. What say you King Cepheus?"

The King could do naught but agree to Fornax's demands. If the world was to be saved then his kingdom must perish. He asked Fornax if none could be saved from the forges?

Fornax relented and said, "One hundred of your people could go forth from the kingdom and be spared."

The King agreed.

Fornax then gave to the King the Sword of Orion. King Cepheus then willed the great sword into the hands of the Titan. With the sword in hand the Titan quickly shattered the Gemstone Demon into a thousand shards of crystal and scattered the pieces across the land. When the battle was finished the Titan returned to the Kings Palace, now encompassed by Cloud Mountain. Of the Wizards that had created the Titan only a handful were still standing. The Titan returned to his place above the Orb and disappeared. The Orb then slowed its spinning and came to rest, back within the claw that held it.

Fornax had given the King seven days with which to select and prepare the chosen ones for their journey through life. Most of the Wizards that had fallen had died. Their minds consumed in the vast power of the Orb. There were few left to give council to the King in his hour of need. The general population could not know of his pact with Fornax. While the hundred were being chosen the people were told only that they would be representing the kingdom on a mission of grave importance. The first two Wizards chosen to go forth as part of the hundred with the others were named Aka'r and the other Fal'r. Both of these men you have met."

Shielka reeled under the knowledge she was being given. She just couldn't believe it was true.

"What those men have gone through to rebuild their home and country was incredible", she thought.

She felt so sorry for them and was ashamed at what they must think of her and her taking of the Orb.

Maraka continued with the history of the Orb, "Another person you have met was here at the time of the devastation. I, Maraka, Warrior of Apollo, Captain of the Imperial Guard of King Cepheus, I too was here."

Shielka fell back as she felt the impact of Marakas' words flow into her mind. Now the ancient stories of Maraka the warrior came flowing back to her. This was just too much for her mind to take and she was overwhelmed into unconsciousness.

CHAPTER 10: THE DEMON FORTRESS

The Isle of the Kanji had proven to be a prime base for the Demons to operate. Not only had the sinking of the Isle of the Ikano killed most of the Kanji warriors, but a large portion of their Seers as well. The tidal wave that was created and the aftershocks that continue to pound the island chain have kept the other island villagers from traveling across the seas. This allowed the Demons to carry out their plans in total isolation.

Balar is the current leader of the Demons. She planned her strategy in conquering this world over the past several hundred years. So far her plans are all working flawlessly. Her predecessor had been defeated by King Cepheus and it was a long hard battle for her to assert her supremacy over the others of her kind. In the history of demons none have been so malicious or sadistic as Balar the Depraved.

Balar had ordered that a fortress be constructed on the island of the Kanji in a similar fashion to human strongholds. This structure would be immense when completed. The Kanji people who were now slaves to the demons were the primary builders, but as the Kanji were too few to carry out the building of this fortress in a quick manner, the demons raided other islands for their strong and able bodied workers. Soon the entire island chain had been enslaved. All people that showed any sign of the Power were killed or imprisoned. Balar would risk no revolt with these people.

"We would easily win of course, but then who would build my temple fortress if the humans are all dead?" she thought.

Eventually, Balar began sending out search parties to the islands further out and also to the continent. She had expected to find great cities and power centers on the mainland but only found small towns and hamlets instead.

"This is very odd," she thought, "the great Kingdom of Cepheus should have flourished and spread to these shores by now. Very odd, very odd indeed."

Her spies reported from the continent but they brought no word or even mention of the great Kingdom. For the first time in her long cruel life Balar was in doubt. This was beyond anything she had planned or made provisions for.

"Could they know that I have come and are keeping silent?", she thought, "no, if they knew I was here they would be in a panic, fleeing for their lives."

She decided to halt her invasion plans for now, seeking to find out the answer to this enigmatic puzzle before proceeding with her conquest. For it is better to know your enemy and plan ahead, then to blindly go forth unprepared.

Her minions crept about the countryside gathering information and occasionally had some fun with the local townspeople. Soon the word began to spread that demons were about. Most people dismissed these warnings as childrens stories and over imaginative minds.

But a very few listened and wept. For these few people had kept the old stories alive and believed in them and the terrible meaning of what was happening. These were the descendants of the original one hundred of the Kingdom of Cepheus.

After they were sent from the kingdom, the hundred traveled great distances and sang the praise of their kingdom. After several years had passed some longed to return home to their families. Since there was no order that forbid them from returning they did so. They were joyous and full of reverie during the long journey back to the Kingdom. But as they grew closer to the heart of the Kingdom their hearts grew tired and their bodies weary. For when they returned they found nothing but empty houses and buildings, cold monuments to where a proud and noble people once lived. Most of the hundred remained and vowed to rebuild their homeland. Those that chose to leave promised to remember their brethren and to return if ever called upon. But to stay at this time was just too painful.

There was now an immense mountain where the Kings palace had once been. During an exploration of this strange mountain a small cave entrance was discovered. Upon further examination they realized that the palace was in fact still intact and it had been swallowed up by the mountain and buried deep within it. There was some minor structural damage but all in all it was in remarkable shape.

That's when the people decided to rebuild their Kingdom underground. The crops would still be harvested above ground but for the most part the people would find safe refuge beneath the earths surface. For those that practiced the elusive art of magic there was another discovery, they had practically stopped aging. They had suspected as much from the first day that they left the kingdom but passed it off as unreal. But now it was all too obvious. What was a year to the others was less than a month to the wizards.

This was both a curse and a blessing for the people. It was a curse on those magic users who now had to watch as their friends, lovers and family died around them. And it was a boon to the ordinary people who could now benefit from the wisdom and power that these magic users had attained and continued to attain as the ages crept slowly by.

CHAPTER 11: THE DISCOVERY

When Shielka awoke she found that she was lying under a clear sky filled with billions of stars.

"Beautiful," she said softly.

The moon was one quarter full.

"A good sign," she thought.

She looked about but it was difficult for her to see anything. There were trees and bushes scattered about which seemed to move under the light of the moon. It suddenly seemed a very eerie place. She now noticed how cold it was and she was hungry. She couldn't even remember the last time she had eaten. She looked for her pack but it wasn't there. She had left it in her haste to explore the caves.

Shielka heard a soft thumping noise, like someone or something walking on hard ground. Whatever it was, it was getting closer. Shielka cast a spell to softly illuminate the area that she heard the noise coming from. When she did so the beast that was walking by became frightened and upon seeing Shielka charged at her. Shielka would not have believed that a creature so short and stocky could move so quickly. Shielka dove to the left, hit the ground and then jumped up to face the creature as it crashed by where she had stood only a moment before.

The animal was short but wide with a curved tusk on either side of its short snout. It made loud grunting noises as it charged once more. Shielka dove and rolled again keeping clear of the creatures sharp tusks. As the beast turned to make another pass, Shielka called upon her powers to kill the creature. With the completion of that simple thought Shielka extended her left hand toward the creature and five bolts of energy shot from her fingers. They slammed into the creature throwing it back several yards by the force of the blast.

It lay motionless on its back and Shielka began to approach it. Suddenly she stopped.

"I need not get any closer to investigate this beast, I am a Seer," Shielka thought.

With that realization Shielka used her mental abilities to probe the beast to see if it was still alive, it wasn't. Shielka then used her heightened senses to scan the area for more intruders. She detected many small animals but no other large creatures. Shielka cleared some grass and brush away and made a small fire pit. She willed a small fire to come into being near the beast. As she set about cleaning the animal and preparing to cook it Shielka thought about what she had just done.

That was the second time that she had killed. The first was the Demon and now this beast.

"It is too easy to kill", she thought, "I am going to have to be more careful in stressful situations."

While Shielka was eating she became aware of someone approaching. Quickly she moved away from her small fire and hid in a clump of trees. She knew the direction that the intruder was coming from so it was easy to spot his approach. He was a man of medium height and very slender build. He facial features were difficult to see but they seemed unusually sharp or chiseled, unlike any other man she had seen before.

He held a short sword in his right hand and the top of a bow could be seen strung over his shoulder. He approached the camp cautiously, circling around the outer edge of the firelight. He kept his stance low and ready to fight.

He called out then, "Come on out! Your dinner is going to burn, I won't harm you."

He spoke with a strange sing song accent, his voice was high pitched almost like a child. Shielka kept quiet.

The man continued to circle the camp until he found the spot where Shielka had been sitting. He then looked at the ground that led to where she was hiding, it was as if he could follow her very footsteps in the grass. He held out his sword and seemed to say something, a brilliant white light then streaked from his sword and grew into a large globe which engulfed the trees around Shielka. Shielka was blinded for a moment but willed the light to be gone and as quickly as it had appeared the light vanished.

Shielka then searched for the man with her mind but could not find him.

"Impossible", she thought, "how could he hide his mind so completely?"

She then used her talents to cause the noise of someone running away to be heard off to her left. She then heard the sound of someone following her auditory illusion. As her eyes readjusted to the firelight she was amazed to see the man still in the camp. He must have known it was an illusion and had sent one of his own.

"But he is obviously a fighter, how could he use the power", Shielka wondered.

Then he called out again, "Sorry about the light. I didn't mean to frighten you. That was quite a trick you just tried. But next time don't make the running noise quite so loud. The ground here is too soft for footfalls to make that much noise."

He removed his pack and pulled out a water skin. He cut some meat off the creature that Shielka was cooking and began eating. Shielka was a bit annoyed by this but she had no reason to kill him, yet.

He called out once more, "Come on out woman, you have no reason to fear me. I know you are a woman because a man would not have cleaned the beast with the care and precision that I see here. You are a sorceress are you not? So what do have to fear from a simple fighter?"

Shielka responded, "A simple fighter does not cause the sun to appear in the middle of the night. Get out of my camp and find your own food."

The man chuckled and said, "Would you really turn away a weary traveler on a cold night such as this? And all of this food, surely your appetite could not be that big. There is enough here for 10 or 15 of your kind."

Shielka cast some protective spells on herself and stepped out from behind the trees and began moving cautiously toward the camp. As she did so the man set down his food and nervously watched her approach.

"For her to have dispelled my magic this must be a powerful sorceress", he thought, "perhaps she knows something of my quest?"

Shielka spoke, "You may share my camp for a meal but then you must go. But before you go tell me who you are and where it is you are going and why you travel at night. Speak truthfully for I will know if you lie."

"Wait a minute, slow down, one question at a time please. My name is Talos and I come from the tree city of Evergreen. I am on a quest. I travel at night because there are those that would block my way, and travel at night is more easily concealed.

Shielka was about to answer when she felt a cold wind that sent chills up her back.

"Listen," she said, "move away from the fire, quickly."

She then willed the fire to go out. They moved toward where she had hidden before. Listening to the silence that had enveloped the forest they heard the soft sound of something flying through the air above them. As they peered

43

into the darkness they could see a large black object circling overhead. The stench it gave off was almost unbearable. Shielka knew at once what it was, and so apparently did Talos.

He whispered under his breath, "stay down, they've found me again."

Shielka was surprised to hear him comment so unemotionally like that.

"He's fought these Demons before", she thought.

He had his sword in hand now and moved silently away from where Shielka stood. The Demon sensed their presence but something was interfering with his locating their exact position. As the Demon flew lower and prepared to land, Talos swung his sword and struck it from behind. The Demon screamed its rage and whirled about to face its attacker. Shielka had difficulty seeing and she willed her vision to adapt to the darkness. The world seemed to turn a dark reddish color and the figures of the trees and bushes took on an eerie glow. Talos and the Demon stood out strongly in her sight as bright red images fighting in a sea of crimson.

Shielka was enthralled by what she saw. Talos was moving with a skill and grace that she had never seen before.

"Now here is a man that was born to wield a sword", she thought.

Each time the Demon moved in to attack, Talos was able to fend it off. All Shielka could do was stare at the spectacle taking place before her. Then Shielka felt the tingling sensation from her ring and knew it was a warning. Frantically she scanned the sky with her new found night vision but could see nothing. She was about to send her mind forth when she finally saw it. It was a very small Demon, barely as high as her waist, with a long spindly tail. It was creeping up behind Talos.

"I have to warn him", she thought. "No!, I don't have to warn him... I'll attack it."

Shielka called upon the powers of the Earth to feed her strength and then she fired a burst of energy from her right hand toward the small creature. The area around the little Demon erupted into a mass of flames and debris flew in every direction from the blast. Talos and the Large Demon were surprised by the explosion. Unfortunately, the Demon recovered first and leapt upon Talos. Then Shielka noticed that the small Demon was still alive and was moving toward her.

"What have I done?", she thought.

Then her mind reeled under the stress of the situation. She instinctively called upon the power of the earth and sky to protect her and at once she started to glow. Energy crackled from her arms, legs and head. The very air around her began to smolder. The Orb was adding some power to her as well, seeking an opportunity.

The little demon sank back in fear and then flew away as it felt its life forces being sucked out of it. Talos and the large Demon were almost wrestling now and the Demon had a huge advantage. Its clawed hands were ripping the flesh from Talos and all he could do was try to push it away and run.

Then Talos felt it. It was like an icicle being driven deep into his soul. He thought he was dead. The Demon felt it as well and howled an awful wailing sound. Shielka stretched out her hand and a thin ray of white energy shot forth. It encompassed the Demon and lifted it high into the air. Shielka let out a gleeful maddening laugh and with a twist of her hand send a ripple of energy riding along the beam. When the ripple struck the Demon it exploded into ball of intense white light. Shielka laughed, a full bodied insane laugh, and stared across at Talos. Talos' eyes were wide with wonder at what he had just witnessed, but he was too wounded to do anything but collapse onto the cold ground.

The madness that had come over Shielka went away immediately as she watched Talos fall. She ran to where he fell and placed her hands upon his wounds. She willed them to close but nothing happened.

"It has to work!", she cried, "it has to work."

Then she noticed the medallion around Talos' neck, it was faintly glowing in the darkness with a magical light. She had seen similar symbols in Aka'r's cave. She carefully reached out, removed the necklace and tried to close his wounds again. This time it worked. Talos' injuries quickly closed and she fed him her energy to bring him back from near death.

The little Demon that had fled when Shielka began absorbing energy was quite a distance away before it stopped flying. When it was sure that it hadn't been followed it set out to return to its master.

Garnath was a powerful Demon lord. It liked using the little Imps for scouts as they were easily terrified and therefore easily controlled. Garnath was intrigued by the report that the Imp gave. This human woman displayed powers that he hadn't heard about in centuries.

"I have to meet her," he howled.

Garnath then gathered a few of his most powerful Demon guards and headed for where Shielka and Talos were last seen.

CHAPTER 12: THE SEARCH

Aka'r and Fal'r were in the old Kings library studying the ancient texts in search of answers to questions as yet unasked.

"What was that?", Aka'r said.

"What was what?", said Fal'r jumping to his feet.

"Calm down my friend", Aka'r replied, "I was just thinking about something I saw as I left the Guardian Chamber. There was a staff laying there. Shielka must have dropped it. Maybe we can find out more about her by examining it."

"We examined it before, it and her dagger. Nothing unusual about them", said Fal'r.

"Perhaps we missed something, we didn't know she could control magic before either."

"You're right, let's go see what we can discover", Fal'r said as he headed for the door.

"Wait Fal'r, you must stay here and rest. Besides you spend more time here then I do and know how to research these things better then anyone. I will retrieve the staff while you see if you can find out anything more about the Demons."

"Alright," said Fal'r, "But be careful."

Aka'r traveled down the many passages from the library to where the Orb had been kept these past few centuries and he thought of Shielka.

"Why did she do it?", he wondered aloud.

Nothing she had done or said had prepared him for the current situation. He reached the spot where Kondore had been chained and saw the staff. It was a fine piece of workmanship. He had never seen that type of wood before and he wondered now why he had not noticed its unusual nature earlier. He cast a spell to see if in fact it was magical. The aura that the staff gave off nearly blinded him.

"The power that is stored within this staff must be immense", he thought, "I must get this to Fal'r right away."

He reached out his hand to pick up the staff and abruptly jerked his hand away.

"What if it is possessed?", he thought.

So instead of touching it he cast a spell to see if it had a mind or spirit of its own, his spell returned nothing but emptiness.

"Either it is just a very powerful magic staff or there is something hiding within that can shield itself from my spells", he said.

Not wanting to take any unnecessary chances he cast a spell that created an energy field under the staff and lifted it into the air. The energy field carried the staff along the passageways slightly behind Aka'r. He traveled at a brisk pace along the winding corridors until he finally returned to the library.

Fal'r put on a wide grin as he saw the staff following behind Aka'r.

"What's the matter Aka'r, scared of a little stick in your old age?"

Aka'r returned Fal'r's question with a laugh and said, "My old age? If we weren't so busy I'd show you something about age. Have you found anything that can shed some light on what's been happening?"

"Nothing yet. But something is bound to turn up. There is always a pattern to history, always. We just have to look more closely that's all. After all, the failures and tragedy of the past are doomed to be repeated unless we find the pattern and prepare for it."

"Or avoid it altogether," replied Aka'r.

Aka'r caused the energy field holding the staff to put it down lengthwise upon one of the large reading tables. Fal'r stepped closer for a better look but then hastily moved away.

"No. It can't be."

"What?" asked Aka'r.

Then as if a man possessed, Fal'r blankly walked over to a wall of books and levitated up to the ceiling. There, on the top shelf, was a dusty old tome with a cracked leather cover and broken binding. Fal'r reached out, grabbed it, then gently floated back to the ground.

"Your ability to find things that you have seen only once will never cease to amaze me my friend."

Fal'r came back to his senses and laid the book down next to the staff. Gently he opened the book and gingerly turned the pages. Some dust blew up into Aka'r's face and Aka'r quickly stifled a sneeze.

"Couldn't you at least have cleaned it off first?", said Aka'r.

Before Fal'r could answer Aka'r went into a fit of sneezing. Aka'r was jumping around the room he was sneezing so hard.

Fal'r could only offer his sympathy and apologies.

"Sorry", Fal'r said, "I forgot you were allergic to dust again."

Another few sneezes was the response.

After a short while Aka'r quit sneezing and Fal'r pointed to a page in the book. There was a drawing of a slender magic wand that had the identical markings as those that were on Shielka's staff.

"This is a picture of the Wand of Oralin. It was created and used by the great Master Mage Oralin eight hundred years ago. He created it as a purely offensive weapon and used it against the evil creatures of this world. According to this book, the wand had the power to cast a great number of spells and recharge itself through absorbing the energy of enemy spells. It was ideally suited to long range combat as the offensive capabilities included shooting fireballs, lightning bolts, cold beams, that sort of thing. It could also cause fire to rain down from the sky, cause earth quakes, hailstorms and a host of other disasters. It was a powerful weapon indeed," said Fal'r.

"All of that from a single wand?" asked Aka'r, "I've had my share of magic wands that could cast fireballs and lightning. And I've used many powerful magic items in my life, but I have never even thought that it was possible to harness all of that diverse energy into a single device."

Then Aka'r noticed Fal'r staring at the staff as it lay on the table.

"If what you read could truly be contained by Oralin in that wand, then what powers could he have projected into the staff. And 'how' Fal'r, did Shielka obtain such a weapon?"

"The book mentioned that there was a rumor of Mage Oralin working on a staff at the time of his disappearance. But nothing was ever found. Mage Oralin just dropped out of sight long ago. Nobody has seen or heard of him in centuries. As to how Shielka may have obtained it? I don't know. It appears though that she did not know the staff's full potential or she wouldn't have needed to fight with Kondore."

"Well this is getting us nowhere. I'm going to ask it directly."

"You can't. You are too important here for me to allow you to do this."

"Allow me to do this? I've had more experience than you and there is no one else."

The spell was easy enough to cast but it was risky if the staff was indeed possessed. As Aka'r prepared himself, Fal'r set about making the protective circles around Aka'r to protect him from anything attacking his mind while he was communicating with the staff.

As Aka'r spoke the final words of the spell, Fal'r was very tense and nervous. If something went wrong and Aka'r did lose his mind to the staff then Fal'r would have to destroy Aka'r's body. This would prevent the mindless body from destroying the mountain and the kingdom.

Aka'r's mind floated now. He could see the essence of the staff and it was alive. It had been able to use its awesome power to prevent his spells from seeing it. But now they were on the same plane of existence and he saw it clearly. A pulsating star within the center of the staff.

Cautiously he called out to it, "I bring greetings to the great Staff of Oralin."

Surprisingly the staff answered, "Greetings Aka'r of Ribald."

Aka'r was stunned as the staff mentioned the name of the town in which he was first born. Not even Fal'r knew that.

"Can you, no, will you aid us in the fight against the Demons?"

The staff responded cryptically, "I was created to be a defensive weapon. I cannot use my powers against those that have not attacked. Only those that attack can be defended against."

"What are your powers?", asked Aka'r.

"My powers are your powers and yet they are not. My range is the length of your arm and yet it is not. That which will defend is what I become and yet I stay the same. When used properly none may attack my master and yet my master may die. Such has been the way of my power and yet it need not be so."

Aka'r was more than a little confused, but he reasoned that what the staff said had been a yes.

"What are the words of command that will allow you to use your powers against the evil ones", Aka'r inquired.

"I protect when I am called to protect", was all the staff said.

Aka'r was getting a little weary and decided to return to his body. Fal'r watched carefully as he saw Aka'r's body move once more. Fal'r could see that Aka'r was tired but that everything was all right.

"What happened," asked Fal'r.

Aka'r relayed his experiences to him and Fal'r's eyebrows dipped low on his forehead as Aka'r spoke. Then as Aka'r told of what the staff had said Fal'r's expression changed.

"The staff speaks in riddles", Fal'r said joyously.

Fal'r loved a good riddle and by what Aka'r had just said, Fal'r could release his fear of the staff.

"But we still haven't learned anything about Shielka", Aka'r said.

As soon as Aka'r spoke Shielks' name the tip of the staff began to glow. Aka'r and Fal'r moved away from the table. The staff then began to move. It began to rotate upon its center. It rotated about thirty degrees to the left and then the tip began to pulsate with an eerie green light. Aka'r and Fal'r stared at it for a few moments.

Fal'r thought for a few more moments and said, "Shielka!"

The staff grew brighter.

"This is great", it's like a Magical Location Arrow. Now we can track down Shielka and retrieve the Orb.", Fal'r said excitedly.

Aka'r was not as easily convinced.

"How do we know that it is pointing to the same Shielka that we are talking about? How do we know that the staff isn't pointing to an enemy?"

Fal'r impulsively reached out and grasped the staff with his right hand.

Aka'r yelled, NO!"

Immediately Fal'r felt the immense power that was contained within the staff. The power flowed into him like a river flows over a waterfall. But he was a master of his craft and could not be so easily consumed.

Fal'r called the staff to life, "lead us to Shielka."

It pulled him around and faced the south west wall of the library and started forward dragging Fal'r behind. As the staff was about to reach the wall Aka'r cast a spell to hold Fal'r in place. But the energy of his spell was absorbed by the staff and had no effect.

Fal'r seeing himself about to smash into the wall yelled, "Staff Stop!", and the staff stopped.

"Don't ever be so impulsive as to do that again under a hundred feet of solid rock. At least wait until we get outside, okay?"

Fal'r just nodded and began the long walk to the surface. As he and Aka'r walked along, Aka'r called out "Ding'ger, come!" Ding'ger loved the surface and howled with joy at the opportunity to hunt there again.

CHAPTER 13: THE DEMON QUEEN

As Zak prepared to enter the Demon Queens chambers he heard her fury being directed at another one of her generals. Then a massive blast rocked the citadel and Zak thought, "there goes another general."

Balar seemed to take great pride in destroying her assistants for the slightest transgression. Zak made sure that if there was ever bad news to be delivered than someone else would deliver it. He always showed up with good reports. Even if they weren't true they were at least good.

Zak pounded the heavy iron doors and called out,"Balar, it is I, General Zak."

He then entered to see the last bit of smoke clearing from the room. The smoke that could have been him if he were not so smart.

"I bring good news my Queen", Zak said with a low bow.

Balar loved the way of human royalty. It was so orderly and utterly ruthless. As the ruler she was given absolute power over her subjects. Anything she said or did was considered as law. In the realm of Demon Kind this type of power was the same but it was harder to assert. But here upon this plane it was the accepted order of things and her Demon servants readily accepted it. They either accepted it or were sent back to perish in flames for a thousand years.

"Being Queen is so much fun", she thought.

Zak continued, "I have located the Half Elf Talos."

Balar spun around and faced Zak at the mention of her most hated enemy. "Silence!", she yelled, "How dare you mention that creatures name in my presence?"

"I only thought to give you some sport my Queen. One of my scouts encountered him. He almost retrieved him for your pleasure but something happened."

She glared at him and said, "What do you mean almost brought him back?"

"My scout was sending his report telepathically as they were fighting when suddenly the communication ended. I have checked our home on the Demon world and all of the dimensional barriers and my scout has just vanished."

"You mean the poor wretch has been banished", Balar said.

"No my Queen, my scout has ceased to exist completely."

"Demons don't just cease to exist. They get banished here or there, they just don't disappear forever."

"There has been one other instance my Queen. On the Island that you sank, on the Isle of the Ikano, there was one of us that ceased to be. His screams of agony still echo throughout the ether. Could it be that someone from that Isle still exists? Could the Maraka of old still be alive?"

"No, even Maraka did not have the power to destroy Demonkind. There must be something else. Where was Talos last seen?"

Zak thankful to still be among the semi-living quickly replied, "He was seen in the foothills of a valley, in the shadow of a single great mountain."

Zak knew the look of fear quite well. But the one place that he never dreamed of seeing it was on his Queens face, and yet there it was. He saw it the moment he described the location that Talos was last seen.

The Queen stood up again and asked in very even tones, "Are, you, certain?"

"Yes my Queen, I am certain."

"Does anyone else know of this."

"No my Queen, since my scout is gone only you and I know of it."

"Good, speak of this to no one or you'll feel my wrath for eons to come."

"Yes my Queen, your will is my command."

"Yes... I know."

Oh how she loved being a Queen here on Earth.

Zak let out a sigh of relief as he left the Queens chambers. He was lucky to have gotten out of there was his skin intact, literally.

"What was the significance of the area around where Talos was found?", he thought.

Zak was still amazed by the Queens reaction.

"If it was bad enough for her to show fear then I don't want any part of it. But then again if I could control something that the Queen feared then I could rule in her place. No, on second thought, I would still have to deal with Garnath and Garnath wouldn't have any such fears of this mountain I'm sure if it."

Zak then began to think of how he could gain the favor of his Queen by gathering information for her about this mountain. She already knew more about it then he did, that was certain. But his Demon band of spies were the most disciplined and elite of the entire Demon army. They were not seen when they traveled and they only killed on orders.

No unnecessary killing to draw attention to their presence. That was the rule. Any of his Demons caught breaking the rule was banished immediately without appeal or trial.

Zak's word was law to those under his command.

"Yes", Zak thought, "these humans knew how to rule with an iron fist or in the case of Demons, with an iron claw."

Zaks laughter could be heard for a long way off...

Balar sat upon her throne worried and angry. She had learned earlier that the Kingdom of Cepheus had been destroyed by a great mountain created by the Gemstone Demon centuries before. Nothing remained of it but a small village that now grew crops and such. She had restarted her plans for the conquest of this world and did not want to stop again. She was breaking her first rule of combat and it worried her.

"Know your enemy... How many times have I had that drilled into my head? Two Demons have been utterly destroyed and I do not know how it was done. I never even thought it was possible. There has to be a connection between the two occurrences. If there was someone or something on the Island that did escape the destruction, then why did it flee to the old Kingdom? Talos knows that I have returned and he seeks help there, that is understandable. But what is this new force that I must now do battle with? If it combines forces with Talos then there could be serious consequences. On the other hand, if it joins with me then my victory would be assured."

"Zak!", she bellowed, her voice reverberating throughout the palace.

Zak heard her voice and it filled him with fear.

"She usually only yells like that when she is about to torch somebody. But then again maybe it's about Talos."

He flew at top speed across the top of the palace to land upon the terrace of her throne room.

"You summoned me my queen?", he asked with a low bow.

"Of course I summoned you, you idiot, is there anyone else here named Zak?"

Zak knew better then to answer. He just stood there in silence bowing.

"I want you to personally go to that mountain and get Talos. Bring him here to me and bring him to me alive. Do you understand? Alive."

Now it was Zak's turn to show fear. He knew that whatever had destroyed the other two Demons was somewhere around that mountain. He also knew that Talos was one of the most powerful fighters that the Demons have ever faced.

Hesitantly he replied, "I am indeed honored that you would choose me to go out on this important mission, but surely my council is needed here close to my Queen. I will send my best officers out to bring back Talos immediately."

Then after so saying Zak began to leave the room.

"Stop!", screeched Balar, "How dare you speak to me of council and being needed! I decide who is needed and where, not you."

Flames started to rise up from her body scorching the throne behind her.

"If you weren't the very best I'd fry you for lunch. Now get out and bring me Talos! Now!", Balar roared.

Zak half ran and half flew to the terrace and leapt off into the night air. He was very confused now. He had managed to anger the Queen twice in the same day and live. Something was really unusual here for her to be acting so crazy. Not that he was complaining, after all he was still alive, but she was just acting too strangely.

Zak thought about the Demons that he had already sent out to bring Talos to their Queen. Zak hoped that they would succeed in finding him before Zak arrived at the mountain. He still remembered the look of fear on his Queens face when he told her where Talos was. Every time he thought of it, it made him afraid as well.

CHAPTER 14: ELF ?

Shielka had assisted the healers of her village many times in the past. But she had never actually had to heal anyone by herself before. She knew how to close the horrible wounds that were inflicted upon Talos, that was the easy part.

"How do I stop the infection or poisons that the Demon must have carried", Shielka thought.

Talos began to stir under Shielka's hands. Shielka was amazed at the will power and strength of this man. Few among the warriors of her home would have regained consciousness this soon after being so close to death. Talos was painfully aware that he was still alive although he didn't know how. The last thing he remembered was the Demon tearing him apart.

"No", he thought, "it flew off of me."

Then he remembered Shielka glowing in the darkness, a look of joyous madness upon her face and then the Demon exploding in the air.

"Shielka!", he yelled as he suddenly sat upright.

This was a mistake. The pain that shot through his head and body was unbearable and he collapsed back onto the ground.

"Be still", Shielka whispered to him. "You are very badly injured and I can only do so much to help you."

"Potion", Talos said weakly, "red bottle... will help."

Shielka tried to keep Talos still but he was doubled over in pain now. His stomach muscles were pulled tight and he couldn't straighten out.

"A potion in a red bottle?"

She looked around for Talos' pack. She spotted it near where they had been hiding. Quickly she ran to where it lay and opened it.

As she peered inside the pouch she couldn't see anything within it, but it was heavy. She put her hand into the pouch and quickly withdrew it.

"Impossible."

Her hand went into the pouch past her elbow.

"Some type of power made the pouch much larger on the inside then on the outside."

Pushing aside her fear she placed her hand into the pouch as far as it would go. She felt all kinds of items and began pulling them forth. There was gold and silver, various gemstones, a few daggers in very ornate sheaths, some rings and necklaces and on and on. Shielka threw down the pouch in disgust.

"I'll never find anything in this mess."

Picking up the pouch again she yelled at it, "All I want is the stupid red potion you stupid pouch."

After so yelling she felt the pouch stir in her hand and quickly dropped it. Then reaching into the pouch again she felt the narrow neck of a slim vial.

"Of course", she said feeling rather inept, "With this much stuff in the bag you would have to be able to just ask for what you wanted to come out, or you would never find anything."

Carefully she pulled the red vial out of the pouch. It was rather small, only a hand long and a thumb wide. There was a wax seal on one end with a symbol of a smiling face etched into it. She ran back to where Talos was and cradled his head in her lap. She broke the smiling seal on the bottle and was immediately aware of a sweet, honey like smell. She put the bottle to Talos' lips and began to pour. The potion was a lot thinner than she had anticipated by the smell and some of it ran down the side of his face. Carefully she tried again and was able to get most of it into his mouth. Almost immediately Talos began to relax. His face no longer showed the lines of intense pain that his injuries were causing. Shielka noticed that even the scars that were left upon him after she had closed his wounds were now beginning to fade.

"Incredible", she thought.

Then Talos opened his eyes. His first reaction upon seeing Shielka was to tense up, but then he slowly relaxed.

"Thank you Shielka."

Shielka looked sorrowfully down at him as tears began to form in her eyes and said, "I'm sorry Talos, I shouldn't have tried to attack that little creature. I distracted you and the Demon took advantage of that. You could have been killed and it would have been my fault.

Talos didn't know what to say. He had thought that the Demon had caused the blinding flash of light.

"It's okay Shielka", Talos said warmly. "It wasn't your fault. You had know way of knowing that some of these creatures have a very high resistance to magic. I am alright now and the Demons have been banished, that is the main thing."

"My talisman!", he said clutching at his throat, "Where is it?"

Shielka was startled by his sudden outburst and just pointed at the ground where it lay.

Quickly he put it on and asked, "How long have I been without it?"

"Not long, a few minutes."

"They will know where we are now", he said flatly.

"I had to remove it for my healing powers to work", Shielka quickly explained.

Talos looking at her and noting her anguish replied, "I see, and thank you again."

Shielka was visibly amazed that Talos had fully recovered so quickly.

"The healing magic of these people is amazing", she thought.

Talos went over to where his pouch was and noted his possessions scattered all over the ground. He turned to Shielka and asked, "Don't you know about such things as this pouch?"

Shielka not knowing what else to say simply replied, "I do now."

Talos just didn't understand this woman. She had to be the most powerful Sorceress that he had ever seen or heard about.

"How can she not know about magic Bags of Infinite Holding?", Talos thought, "For someone to be so powerful and yet so inexperienced in magic is a dangerous thing."

"What did you do to the little Demon?", Talos asked.

"What?"

"The little Demon you mentioned, what did you do to it?"

"Nothing. I tried to kill it but it deflected the blast. Then I saw the large Demon leap upon you and the little one advancing toward me and I think I panicked. I kind of remember a floating sensation and then killing the Demon that was upon you. I don't remember doing anything to the little one. It must still be around here!"

Talos said a few words that were foreign to her and slowly turned about in a full circle. "It is not nearby. But I have a feeling that they will be here soon and in force. Lets go quickly."

"Where to?", Shielka asked.

"You tell me, this is your home."

"This way", she said moving in what she hoped was the direction of the mountain.

Shielka didn't know where else to go but back to Cloud Mountain.

"Hopefully Aka'r will forgive me", she thought as she felt the Orb through its leather sack.

After traveling only a short distance Talos stopped and looked in wonder at Shielka.

"What's the matter?", she asked.

"How can you find your way in this darkness? Is this terrain so familiar to you that you can just feel your way around."

Shielka giggled a little and replied, "I can see in the darkness because I wish to see in the darkness. You seem to have no trouble with the lack of illumination, why then do you expect me to?"

Talos thought for a minute and simply replied, "You are right, forgive me. It is just that I find it unusual for a human to have the ability to see in the dark, that's all. I meant no disrespect."

Shielka moved away from him and asked, "What do you mean, 'unusual for a human'? What are you than if not human?"

Talos laughed aloud with an astonished look upon his face. "I thought you knew", he said.

"Knew what?"

Talos pushed his flowing hair away from the side of his face to reveal pointed ears.

"I am only half human", he replied, "my father was an Elf."

"What's an Elf?", Shielka quickly asked.

Talos was stunned.

"What's an Elf?", he repeated back to her.

"That's right", she said defiantly, "What's an Elf?"

"This is going to take quite some time to explain. Perhaps we had better keep moving along and I will explain on the way."

"Alright."

"The world is populated by many races. On the one hand there are Humans, Elves and Dwarves. With some smaller varieties and combinations thrown in for good measure. For the most part these are counted as the Good races. On the other hand there are Trolls, Goblins and Orcs that generally represent the Evil races. There are many other races living on and under the ground, some good and some evil, but these are the major ones."

Talos went into greater detail about each race and how it began and evolved over the centuries. Shielka was amazed by all of the things on her world that she did not know.

"I have lived my entire life in a cocoon. All I knew was my own people and the islands that we called home. No one ever dreamed that all of these other creatures could exist."

Talos noticing Shielka slowing her pace suggested that they set up camp and rest.

"No, I'm not tired, we must keep moving and get you to safety."

"We'll, I'm tired," he replied as he sat down on a fallen log.

They were in a small clump of trees now so he reasoned that they could rest for a while and be safe from the Demon spies. He was lying when he told her that he was tired. The potion had completely restored his strength and vitality but he was concerned about Shielka, she didn't look very well.

"I'm sorry, I forgot about your wounds. We should rest a while."

"Shielka, you can use my pack as a pillow and rest your eyes for a few moments if you like.

"Oh well, maybe for just a minute or two"

Shielka was soon fast asleep.

Talos wondered about this strange woman. It was as if she had suddenly appeared upon his world from some other dimension or plane.

"For her to know so little about this world is peculiar to say the least", he thought.

As he watched her sleeping he saw her eyes moving beneath the lids and her muscles twitch periodically.

"Dreaming. I hope they are good dreams Shielka, I hope they are good."

Morning came quickly to their small camp. Shielka awoke to the smell of something cooking. She was surprised to see a small animal being cooked over a tiny smokeless fire. She felt stiff from sleeping on the hard ground and stood up stretching.

"You should have woken me."

Talos merely shrugged his shoulders and replied, "I didn't want to startle you."

Shielka looked around and discovered to her delight that they were in fact closer to the mountain. Talos offered her some of the rabbit and they ate in silence. After breakfast Talos carefully put out the fire. The fire had been created in a small hole that Talos had dug. So when he covered it with dirt he was able to make the spot blend in perfectly with the rest of the terrain. If she hadn't seen the fire with her own eyes she would never have believed that one had ever been there.

Soon after setting out again they saw large masses of smoke coming from over a small knoll to the east. They decided that they had better investigate so whatever caused it would not surprise them from behind on their journey.

When they reached the crest of the hill, they could see wagons burning on the other side. Six wagons in all were crushed and smoldering. A huge reptilian beast was sifting through the wreckage.

"Dragon!", Talos said.

Shielka didn't know why but she was afraid. Then she felt movement at her side. The Orb was spinning within the pouch. The friction against the sides of the bag was causing it to heat up and smolder. Without really thinking about it Shielka reached into the bag to grasp the spinning Orb and stop it from turning. When her fingers touched it the Orb stopped, and so did the Dragon.

68

It was a huge beast, as big as a large house. Talos turned and started to grab for Shielka to tell her to move away and go back down the hill but when he saw her he stopped. She was holding the Orb out at arms length in front of her and she was walking down the hill toward the Dragon. Talos was enthralled by the Orb and his mind reeled. He fell to his knees and looked helplessly on as Shielka walked toward the Dragon and to her doom.

CHAPTER 15: THE SURFACE

Aka'r and Fal'r reached the surface cave entrance to Cloud Mountain and took long deep breaths of the cool night air. The air felt fresh, crisp and clean.

"It has been too long since we have come up here my friend", Aka'r said.

"It seems like years Aka'r, like years..."

There was a sad tone in Fal'r's voice, almost a trembling.

Aka'r thought, "It had been so long ago but he'll never forget what happened, my poor friend."

"Come on Fal'r", Aka'r said loudly as he began walking out of the cave, "Ding'ger come!"

Ding'ger ran out ahead of them almost knocking over the guard at the cave entrance.

"Hey! Watch out!", the guard yelled.

Then as he turned to see who was coming out of the cave he broke into a wide grin.

"Your Majesty!", the guard said while lowering himself onto one knee and bowing deeply.

"Oh, get up", Aka'r said rather annoyed, "I told all of you that I do not accept being made King."

"Yes your majesty", the guard said while keeping his head bowed so that Aka'r would not see him chuckle.

Fal'r didn't hide his mirth and laughed loudly.

Aka'r looked at them both for a moment and started stomping down the hill.

Fal'r said to the guard, "He'll come around eventually you know."

The guard smiled as he stood up and said, "You're next in line Fal'r."

Fal'r's face looked pained as he replied, "Oh no you don't. Aka'r!, wait for me..."

He scurried down the hill after his friend.

Fal'r caught up to Aka'r quite a distance from the cave entrance.

"Wait Aka'r", Fal'r said, "before we get too far lets see what direction she is from us."

They deliberately didn't use Shielkas' name except when they wanted the staff to work.

Aka'r stopped and said, "Yes. You're right. It would be better to begin the search now."

Fal'r still had the staff in hand. Slowly he held it out and said, "Shielka."

The staff responded immediately, its tip lit up with a soft green glow. The staff seemed to know that it was darker out here under the stars than it was in the library and it deliberately gave off less light.

It pulled Fal'r around so that he faced toward the South West and the glow began to pulsate.

"Shielka", Fal'r said again and the staff pulled him forward toward the base of the mountain.

Ding'ger, oblivious to what his masters were doing was jumping around for the sheer thrill of it. Oh how Ding'ger loved to be outside with all of the little animals to hunt and play with.

71

As Fal'r was about to enter the small trees that lined the base of the mountain, Ding'ger suddenly crouched down and froze. Then, almost faster then the eye could follow Ding'ger charged past Fal'r and leapt between the trees and attacked something.

Fal'r commanded the Staff, "Halt" and it did so.

Aka'r readied an offensive spell but didn't cast it for fear of hitting Ding'ger. Fal'r cast a light spell into the woods to get a better view of what was going on. The men were surprised to see that Ding'ger was fighting nothing. She was fighting something but it was invisible to their eyes. Fal'r cast another spell to allow him to see invisible creatures. When he looked again at Ding'ger, he saw that he was fighting with an Orc. Fal'r was amazed by this as he had never seen an invisible Orc before. Fal'r laughed to himself at that thought, "never seen an invisible Orc."

Aka'r called out, "What is it Fal'r?"

"An Orc," Ding'gers fighting an invisible Orc."

"That's strange", Aka'r thought, "when it attacks it should become visible again but it doesn't."

Aka'r pulled a small tube out from his robe and blew into one end. A small cloud of glowing sand was sent forth and some of it found its way onto the Orc. As the sand stuck to the Orc Aka'r could see its outline. Fal'r was content to let Ding'ger kill it but Aka'r was a bit on the humane side at times. Aka'r let loose with a volley of energy bursts. When these energy globes struck the Orc a great shower of sparks erupted. The Orc was no longer standing before them, in its place was a slender Demon.

The Demon laughed as it saw the look of horror on the human faces. But then it howled in pain and fell to one knee as Ding'ger bit a large chunk out of its leg. Aka'r was the first to react with another energy globe spell aimed at the creature. This time though the energy just dissipated harmlessly around it and crashed into a nearby tree utterly destroying it. The Demon got up and jumped toward Aka'r. Aka'r called upon another spell to protect himself and the Demon crashed into an energy barrier. Then quicker than they recalled these monsters to be, the Demon wheeled about and attacked Fal'r.

Fal'r instinctively raised the staff to protect himself and the Demon crashed into it. There was a gigantic explosion.

When Fal'r awoke his head was in Aka'r's lap and Ding'ger was licking his hand.

"What happened?", Fal'r asked.

With a small tear in Aka'rs' eye he replied, "When the Demon leapt upon you, you raised the staff to defend yourself. The staff created an energy field that would have protected you from the Demons attack if it had been a normal one. But since the Demon was actually falling down upon you from the sky its momentum slammed you down onto the ground. This caused the Staff to expend more energy to protect you. The Demon appeared to be stunned by the Staff but since it was still on top of you the Staff kept pouring energy into it. Then there was a colossal explosion and the Demon was gone. Look around you my friend. You are now in a hole as large as the library and about waist deep. I thought that you had been killed for certain."

"Killed? Me? Hah, but I do have the worst headache you could possibly imagine."

Aka'r gave him a healing potion and helped him to sit up.

"Well, the Demons are back that's for certain," Aka'r said.

"But why was that one disguised as an Orc?", Fal'r asked.

Fal'r paused then continued, "Do you think that the Demons are allying themselves with the Orcs?"

"That's rather unlikely. But if they were to disguise one of themselves as an Orc and bully their way to become an Orc leader, that could stir up a lot of trouble for us."

"Another possibility would be if they wanted a spy, than what better disguise than an Orc?", Fal'r commented, "One thing's for certain, she didn't lie to us about the Demons. Aka'r, what if the Demon was looking for her? A Demon hasn't been within a thousand miles of this mountain for centuries. Suddenly she appears, takes the Orb, disappears and then a Demon shows up on our door step. Just a coincidence? I think not. There is something very strange going on here. Something very big and very strange. I feel like a pawn in some great game.

"There is something afoot that's for sure. But a pawn in a game? Who's to say? Right now I think we should move back up to the cave and camp until daylight. It's been a long night."

Ding'ger followed them up the hill toward the cave entrance, guarding the men as they traveled. Ding'ger would occasionally run back down the hill and crisscross their path to see if anything followed them, but tonight all was clear. Ding'ger couldn't see or smell anything unusual. But way off in the distance his keen ears picked up the lonely call of a creature howling at the moon.

CHAPTER 16: FOUND OUT

Zak was flying inland now, low, just above a frothing river. He had brought along his two most powerful Demon warriors, Arnot and Darrow.

Darrow was the larger of the pair at seven feet tall and three feet wide at the shoulder. His barrel like, muscular arms, ended in razor sharp claws that constantly oozed acid from beneath the tips of the three talons. With a large angular face closely resembling that of a bat, it was a hideous creature to behold.

Arnot was a much smaller Demon. Only five feet tall and two feet wide. Its arms ended in hands much like that of a human. What it lacked in strength it more then made up for in speed. It was by far the quickest Demon that Zak had ever seen. Because of its blinding speed it was able to get in, attack and kill its opponents before they even knew they were under attack. Also because if its "hands", it was able to use human weapons. Arnot's favorite weapon was a small hand sickle that it always carried lashed about its waist.

Instead of traveling in a direct path toward the mountain Zak decided to follow along several rivers that flowed through the region. He reasoned that by traveling at night over the water they could stay closer to the ground and avoid detection. Then, even if they were spotted, their course could not be easily plotted. That is what he told his companions, and to some extent he believed that as well. After all it did made good sense. But than again if it took him a little longer to meet up with Talos, so much the better.

As dawn broke and the sun began its slow assent into the azure sky, they headed for a rocky knoll on which to stop for the day.

Zak gave orders to the others to dig a cave for them to sleep in during the day so that they wouldn't be spotted.

After the small cave was ready Zak said rather disdainfully, "It is going to be a clear bright day."

Arnot and Darrow both nodded their dissatisfaction as well. Zak then arrogantly called upon the wind and rain to blot out the sun and bring thunder and lightening to the world. Soon the entire region was covered with an unseasonably heavy rain storm. Thunderclaps could be heard approaching and bolts of lightening could be seen striking the ground nearby.

"That will keep any nosey villagers inside their puny shacks", Zak said aloud.

Again Arnot and Darrow kept silent. They had learned millennia ago that if Zak does not ask you a direct question then do not offer an opinion, on anything.

***

In one of the nearby villages the people were awed by the severity and suddenness of the storm. There had never been a storm like this before, and to come so quickly out of nowhere. They knew that there had to be something unnatural about this gale but they didn't know how to go about finding out exactly what. They needed to be out in the fields getting work done. There had to be some way to combat this torrential rain.

Menja was the current leader of the village. He had been elected to that position many years ago and had enjoyed a peaceful existence, up until now. The people of the village were now calling upon him to do something about their present situation. Rumor already had it that the rain was predicted to last for weeks and if that happened then their entire crop would be destroyed. Menja knew he had to seek help but from where? He was in mid thought when a bolt of lightning struck nearby and let loose with a thunderclap that shook the buildings to their very foundations. A clay flower pot was knocked off of a shelf by the blast and Menja cut himself on the prickly thorns of a holly branch as he foolishly tried to catch it before the pot hit the ground.

"Holly berries", Menja said aloud, "Holly berries."

Years ago one of the young girls in the village was passionately fascinated with helping the living things of the world. She had an uncanny ability to sense when a plant or tree was unhealthy and what to do to heal it. While she was in the village her abilities allowed them to harvest record crops and still maintain a balance with nature. Eventually a small band of Druids came in from the east and spoke to her at great length in private. Shortly after their meeting she left the village to go and live with them. The Druids had dedicated themselves to helping the plants and animals of the world to live in peace and harmony with humans. Always though it was the humans that desecrated the land. The Druids were a solitary people and they did not appreciate unwarranted intrusion but perhaps they would help in this instance.

Menja set out into the pouring rain to find the Druids and ask for their help. Several others from the village went out with him to assist on the journey. After traveling most of the day they suddenly stepped into an area of daylight and calm. They knew at once that they were nearing the Druids as this peaceful calmness was just as unnatural as the storm outside its boundary.

Immediately after Menja and his companions entered the area, a slender man dressed all in green stepped out from within a tree and asked, "Who are you and why did you come to this grove?"

Menja spoke, "I am Menja, leader of the village of Tah. I bring greetings to you and your kin and to the many Druids that reside here. We have come seeking your aid against this foul unnatural weather."

The man in green paused a moment then said, "follow me" and he turned and walked away at brisk pace.

Menja and his men followed.

After a while they came to the base of a very wide and very tall tree.

The man in green said, "wait here", and Menja waited.

After only a short while an elderly man came walking forth from out of the base of the tree. His lily white robes were matched by the long white beard flowing from his chin.

"I am Hawthorne, leader of this Druid settlement. Greetings to you and your people, Menja of Tah. Willow, daughter of the village of Tah, has come a long way since she was accepted as one of us. She does your village great honor", Hawthorne said with respect.

"You honor us by your presence and by your praise of our daughter", Menja replied.

"I believe that your guard has told you of why we have come?", Menja said with a questioning tone in his voice.

"Yes."

Both men now remained silent for a long time.

Hawthorne broke the silence, "Your village has expanded to use a great deal of land. If you want our help then you will have to pay for it."

"What?!?", Menja blurted out, "We are a poor village and you want us to pay for your help? What can we pay? We can barely support ourselves."

Hawthorne appeared not to notice the anger in Menjas voice.

Hawthorne replied, "your village has done well to maintain the balance of nature, but others have not. I would charge your village with the task of educating the other villages in the area about conservation and taking care of the land. In return for that and the agreement of your village to planting one hundred trees on the far side of the river, the Druids will aid you."

Menja hesitated just long enough to be respectful and then said, "Thank you Hawthorne, for your most generous offer. I apologize for my outburst a moment ago but it has been a long and tiring trip for me. The people of Tah gladly accept your offer and will begin a campaign soon to enlighten the other villages to the ways of nature and the land. If you would but provide us with the seeds to begin planting we will begin as soon as the rain is stopped."

Hawthorne called out to the trees, "go get Willow" and a man appeared from out of an Oak tree and ran off into the brush.

Soon a woman stepped out of the Oak tree behind Hawthorne and approached the two men. Menja recognized her immediately. She had grown so much.

"Willow, these men of Tah require our assistance. The crops will soon drown and die in this torrential rain. Go with them and seek out the foul nature of this storm and eliminate it.", Hawthorne commanded softly.

Willow acknowledged the command, turned and headed out the way that Menja had come in. When she saw that she was not being followed she turned and looked at Menja.

"Well? Aren't you coming", she said to him teasingly.

Menja was weary and tired and wanted to rest there for the night, but duty called.

"Yes, yes of course we're coming", Menja hastily replied.

As they broke through the protective barriers that the Druids had erected Menja expected to once again be drenched by the rain. Instead he found that Willow had erected a small shield around them that not only kept out the rain but kept a nice even warn temperature as well. With Willows help they were able to make very good time back to the village. The sun was setting when they entered their village.

Willow set about to work immediately. She could feel the direction that the storm was emanating from and it was a strong supernatural feeling. Whatever had caused it was either close by or very powerful or both. Willow began her enchantments to dispel the storm. To her surprise there was not much difficulty in disbursing it.

Whatever had caused it was not sustaining it with any amount of power so it was easy for her to stop the rains and disburse the clouds.

Zak roared out, "What!?! Who dares to dispel my storm?"

Instantly Zak caused another storm to come into being even stronger then the first. Willow was momentarily stunned by its force as she was taken by surprise. She again cast the enchantments to dispel the storm. This time it took a great deal more of her energy. But again she was able to cause the storm to dissolve into harmless vapor.

Zak was furious.

Yelling to Arnot and Darrow he said, "Find out who's dispelling my magic and kill it."

Immediately they took off into the night sky and searched for the source of energy that combatted their master's will.

Meanwhile, Zak and Willow kept battling over the weather. As this went on, Arnot and Darrow were easily able to zero in and locate the village of Tah. As they descended down into the area screams of terror could be heard from the people that saw them. Their cries and shouts of warning were lost upon Willow as she was too absorbed in her spell casting to hear them. Menja came running into the room where Willow was and grabbed her. Spinning her around to face him. The moment he did so her concentration was broken and a flood of rain cascaded down upon the village. The streets were like small rivers with a torrent of water gushing through them.

"You fool!", she cried out, "look what you've done!"

Menja was about to explain when the side of the building was ripped apart. There in the gaping hole stood Darrow. Menja was frozen by terror, all he could do was stand there with his mouth open, staring at this horrible creature.

Willow tried to cast spells to protect herself but she knew it was for naught. These were not really living creatures so her spells would be useless. She pulled out a small golden sickle from her belt and prepared to do battle with the Demon in front of her. It's too bad that she never noticed Arnot behind her.

It was over in an instant. Willow lay on the floor lifeless. Menja just kept staring straight ahead at the repulsive sight of Darrow, not even noticing Willows fall. Arnot seeing Willows golden sickle and comparing it to his own took it and threw his aside.

"A golden sickle for a golden Demon",he thought to himself. "Come on", Arnot said to Darrow, "our work here is done."

Darrow turned and they both leapt into the storm and headed back toward Zak.

When Menja was found he was still standing there in shock, staring at the huge hole in the wall. Oblivious to everyone and everything, even the body of his dead daughter laying at his feet.

CHAPTER 17: DRAGON

Shielka slowly walked down the hill toward the Dragon below. The Dragon stood up on its hind feet and stared intently at her in silence. Talos could only lay there and watch. It took all of his energy just to remain conscious.

When Shielka reached the bottom of the hill the Dragon was only twenty paces away. Shielka was having difficulty concentrating and her mind went into and out of focus.

She looked up at the Dragon in wonder and thought, "This magnificent Dragon must be in its prime."

Its dark brown hide was full of luster and covered with large interlocking plates protecting it like armor. There was a slight tinge of red to its color but only when the light reflected off of it in just the right way.

The Dragon was examining the girl intently as well. But his mind was having a great deal of trouble focusing.

"Why don't I want to kill this little human?", it thought.

But with that thought came a stabbing pain at the base of its skull. It shook its head wildly back and forth in fury but did not attack.

Shielka seeing the Dragon's movements and the grimace upon its face, felt sorry for the beast and wished it well.

She then spoke to it in a slurred voice, "Oh Great Dragon before me, be at peace. Warmth and comfort should be yours not pain or suffering."

With those words a soft golden light came from the Orb and engulfed the Dragon. The effect was immediate. The Dragon lay down upon the ground and slowly crawled toward Shielka. Its face clearly had an expression of peacefulness.

When its head was just a few yards from Shielkas, the Dragon spoke very slowly in a deep guttural voice, "Never before have I felt this way little one. I, Bedast, now know what you truly are. But I cannot act against you now. It was foretold in our legends, millennia old, that one day the final confrontation would come between Dragon Kind and the little ones of the world. The signal of its coming would be the death and destruction caused again by the Orb of Orion. The result would either be harmony between us for all time or destruction of the weaker. You have trapped me because I was unaware. But your enchantments upon my mind could not stop me from sending word to Dragons everywhere that the time is near. Go ahead and destroy me little one, for your race is not long for this world."

Shielka's mind was still in a euphoric state and it was difficult for her to digest everything that the Dragon said.

A part of her mind did understand and she responded, "Great Dragon Bedast, I have no wish to destroy you. But my mind is controlled as yours is, by the power of the Orb. I see much destruction around you and it fills me with sorrow and anger. Did you kill and then eat the humans that rode in these wagons?"

Bedast let out a kind of repressed chuckle and said, "No little one, there is not enough meat on you little people to make it worth the effort. This is my area of the mountain. I have lived here for centuries and all that pass must pay tribute. This has been the rule for all little ones for ages. This group did not want to pay. They thought to kill me with their puny arrows. They are gone now. I allowed them to take their horses and leave with their lives. I do not know why."

"The Dragons speech is strange, fluid one minute and then short and abrupt the next", Shielka thought as the Dragon spoke.

Talos was beginning to regain some control of his muscles again. He caught bits and pieces of conversation between Shielka and the Dragon but it didn't sound good.

"If I could only get to my Bow", he thought, "I could use a magic arrow and distract it long enough for Shielka to run away."

As he tried to get into a kneeling position he fought against the urge to just curl up into a ball. The amulet around his neck was starting to get very warm and he knew that it was absorbing the magic that was meant for him.

"How much more energy can this necklace take before it just explodes", he wondered.

Talos just couldn't get enough control of his body to do more then just crouch.

"Well, if I can't distract it one way I'll try another", Talos reasoned.

Then using all of his will, he leaned forward and pushed with his legs, sending himself head-over-heals down the hill toward Shielka and the Dragon.

Talos' movement startled the Dragon and it turned quickly to face this danger. Rearing back it inhaled a vast amount of air and prepared to release its breath weapon upon Talos.

Shielka, not knowing what was happening sensed that Talos was in danger and said to the Dragon, "He is my friend! Do not harm him!"

Then there was an intense roar of wind and heat as the Dragon shot a column of flames a hundred feet into the air. It roared its displeasure with a cry that almost deafened Shielka. In that instant an understanding was reached between Shielka and the Dragon. Shielka realized that the

Dragon would not harm her as long as she had the Orb. She had commanded it and it had obeyed. But it did not willingly do so.

"There was something about the Orb that wanted me to confront this Dragon", she thought.

Bedast, on the other hand, was enraged by the fact that he could do nothing against this little one that now controlled him. A Dragon's life was one of freedom. To be a Dragon was the embodiment of what freedom was all about. But now he was no longer in control of his own destiny and the mere thought of that was driving him to the brink of madness.

Talos rolled to a stop near where the Dragon was but neither Shielka nor the Dragon appeared to pay any more attention to him.

"Great", Talos though, "I nearly break my neck rolling down this hill and they don't even notice."

Then Talos got a whiff of burning sulphur and began to worry.

"Did I miss something while rolling down here?", Talos thought.

Shielka spoke again to the Dragon, "Bedast, I will make a bargain with you. In exchange for knowledge and the promise not to kill us I will give you your freedom."

After so saying it was Shielka's turn to feel the pain of the Orb and she fell to one knee crying.

The Dragon looked hatefully down upon her and said, "You can ask anything and I will have to answer. Why do you toy with me so?"

But Shielka didn't answer. She was doubled over in pain.

It was like being hit in the temple with a rock but a hundred times worse.

The Dragon slowly spoke again, "Little one?"

Shielka managed to speak again, crying out she yelled, "I will give him his freedom!"

The pain shot through her temples a second time. Shielka was brought to both knees now but she couldn't release the Orb. Now the Dragon looked interested.

"Could this one be fighting the Orb and feeling the pain as I did?" Bedast thought.

Then it happened as it had happened before. There was a dull pain in her hand that spread quickly through her arm and shoulder. But this time it was competing with pain and not euphoria. Maraka had sensed what was happening but thought that Shielka would be able to handle it. He had not expected her to set the Dragon free. It was beyond what any rational person would do.

"But then, when had Shielka ever been rational", Maraka thought.

He poured what energy he could into fighting the Orb but it was a losing battle. The Orb had now had time to study Shielka and could exert more power over her. In his explanation to her he didn't want to alarm her by telling her everything about the Orb. He had left out a couple of minor details, like the fact that it was alive.

"But it couldn't be helped", he thought, reassuring himself that he had done the right thing, "If Shielka was going to survive this it would all have to come from her now."

Talos ached all over but he was beginning to be able to move again. Slowly at first and then more and more of his body was able to function normally. Even the warmth of his necklace had subsided.

"There's something bad happening", he thought.

When he could finally stand up he turned to face Shielka and the Dragon. He was shocked to see Shielka writhing in pain and the Dragon standing dumbfounded over her. He almost attacked the Dragon but then his senses came into focus a little better.

"The Orb!", he thought, "That is what is causing all of the problems."

Hastily and not even thinking about the Dragon, Talos ran headlong into Shielka trying to force the Orb out of her hands. He knocked her off of her knees and she rolled across the grass but the Orb was still in her hands when she stopped.

She got up looking like a wild woman. Talos froze when he saw her expression. Even the Dragon experienced the deep animal instinct of fear and just stared at her. Shielka had an intense desire now to destroy both Talos and the Dragon. With energy fed from the Orb she began the thought to kill them. But she never completed it as in that instant she blacked out. Her unconscious mind came forth and took control her body. The energy that had been intended by the Orb to kill Talos was sent into the hill nearby causing a massive explosion that rocked the ground and sent debris everywhere. The forces that now battled within her were enormous. But Shielka had trained for years to control such power, and control it she did. Within the depths of her subconscious mind was the secret power to harness all energy of the world, not just that power contained within the Orb.

The Life force of the Orb found a new respect for Shielka and acknowledged her as its master.

"As it was in the beginning, so it is again", the Orb telepathically said to Shielka's mind.

Then the pain was gone and Shielka's mind cleared. She fell to her knees again exhausted by what she had just been through. Talos limped over to her side and gently cradled her in his arms.

Then they remembered the Dragon.

Bedast was confused by what had just happened. His mind was now clear of the euphoria and he could feel his energy returning but he knew not why.

"The little one held my life in her hands and spared me twice!", he thought.

"You have risked much to free me little one. I felt the pain of the Orb and I never would have expected you to live through it. Others of your kind would have bound me in slavery or just killed me. Why then did you spare me?"

Shielka's head was still throbbing and she could barely move but she managed tilt her head back enough to look up at the Dragon. It has been said that the eyes are mirrors of the soul and when the Dragon looked deep into Shielka's eyes he found peace.

"This human loved life and freedom as much as Dragons did. She would give her life rather than see even a Dragon imprisoned", Bedast thought, "A fitting carrier for the Orb of Orion."

Bedast then spoke unto them, "I, Bedast of Dragon Kind, do solemnly swear on the blood of my ancestors that I will not harm you. In all of the centuries of my life I never expected kindness or compassion from a little one. By the sacrifice that I have just witnessed you have now changed my life forever. You asked for knowledge earlier, I now freely give it. What do you want to know?"

The Dragon's words were lost to Shielka as she had faded off into sleep but Talos heard and was amazed.

All of his life he was brought up and told that Dragons were the most absolute Evil creatures on the Earth. Now to find out that it isn't so was beyond belief.

Talos responded to the Dragons words and hoarsely said, "Mighty Dragon, Shielka has suffered much these past few minutes. Her mind was overwhelmed by the forces within. I am afraid that she did not hear your words of kindness. I will make sure that she knows when she wakes up. It was her wish that you be free, so please leave, Bedast."

"I am free", the Dragon responded, "and I wish to remain here for now. When the little one awakens and is fit, then I may take my leave. But then again maybe not, such is the way of freedom. There have been Demons about and I do not think that it would be difficult for them to overpower you... Talos of Evergreen."

Talos gasped in amazement, "How did you know who I am and where I'm from?"

The Dragon just laughed and began shrinking, changing its shape and form.

CHAPTER 18: PREPARATION

As Aka'r and Fal'r approached the cave entrance, several guards came running out to help them. The guard on watch had seen and felt the massive explosion and sounded the alarm.

Fal'r was carried into the cave and placed on a small cot. He was feeling much better now thanks to the healing potion that Aka'r had given him. But it would be a disservice to the people if he didn't let them tend to him for at least a little while. Fal'r endured the questions and the pillow fluffing in good humor.

Aka'r was getting quite a different treatment entirely. His advisors were very politely reprimanding him for going out in the middle of the night alone.

Aka'r responded that he wasn't alone, he had been with Fal'r and Ding'ger.

That comment brought a host of reprisals from those gathered in the room.

"Being with Fal'r and Ding'ger is the same as being alone. How can an old man and an animal protect you?" one of the guards said loudly.

It got deathly quiet.

The expression on Aka'r's face turned from one of playful embarrassment to one of intense rage. Aka'r thought, "Fal'r was almost killed while protecting me and this man dares to call him unfit?"

Aka'r replied, his voice showing evidence of controlled rage, "You dare to question Fal'r's ability? He could cause the flesh to rot from your bones or turn your body to stone. A simple spell could kill all of you in this room. Shall I ask him to demonstrate his ability to protect me by turning you into a slug?"

The guards face turned white with fear. He was new to the ranks of the King's guard and when the others started badgering Aka'r he joined in. The guard dropped to the ground on both knees and said, "Spare me! Spare me! I'm sorry, I have a wife, please spare me. I meant no disrespect."

The others in the room were shocked by what Aka'r had just done. He had never acted this way before. Something must be terribly wrong. The room remained deathly silent.

Aka'r turned away from the guard and said to the Captain of the Guard, "Post two guards at the cave entrance. I want 2 more stationed every 20 yards down the hill. At the bottom of the hill there is a large crater. Four guards should be posted there. Now leave us. We need rest and must set out again at first light. Send for Tama'r and Andromeda. Have them join us in the morning."

"Yes your Majesty" was the reply from the guards and advisors.

When Aka'r and Fal'r were alone again Fal'r spoke, "We need to tell the others."

"Tell them what? Tell them that the Demons have returned? How many Demons? Why have they returned? These will be the first questions they ask us. What will we say? We need more information."

"Tama'r is just a child, a Junior Mage at best. Why are you sending for her help?"

"I hardly think Tama'r could be classified as a child. Yes, her overall performance as a student has been below average in the general studies. And she has not moved beyond the rank of Junior Mage. But, she has excelled at the art of far-seeing. Her ability in this area is without equal. I believe that skill will aid us greatly," Aka'r explained.

"What about Andromeda. She is not the best Healer in the mountain. Nor is she a specialist in Demonology. Why did you choose her?"

Aka'r replied with a grin, "Andromeda and Shielka are about the same age. Andromeda might be a little older. They are both very attractive and energetic. Perhaps they can become friends and Andromeda can convince Shielka to return the Orb. Do not underestimate her abilities as a Healer either. She has come far in her training with Cygnus the past few years."

Fal'r was satisfied with the answers and soon fell fast asleep. Aka'r was not far behind.

Aka'r awoke. The aroma of boar meat frying permeated the air. Someone had made a cook fire near the mouth of the cave. One of the cooks was preparing a large breakfast. There was boar meat frying in one pan and eggs in another. Next to a third pan was a stack of breakfast cakes.

Aka'r wasn't hungry when he initially woke up. But the sight and smell of all that food made him ravenous.

Fal'r began waking up as well but lounged in bed for a moment, savoring the smell of morning cooking. This was his absolute favorite time of day. He could just lie there serene and undisturbed. He would get up at his own pace. Many people have learned their lesson about abruptly awaking Fal'r. Fortunately all survived being changed back into their human forms.

Aka'r called to his friend to wake up and eat. It was time to get moving.

A hot spiced cinnamon-apple drink was served with the meal. Aka'r did not care for the morning drink that most of the people consumed. It was stimulating, but too bitter for his tastes.

As Aka'r and Fal'r were finishing their meal, Tama'r and Andromeda came walking up the stairs.

In unison they bowed to Aka'r and said "Good morning your Majesty."

Aka'r just gave them a stern look, shook his head, and said softly to himself "I give up..."

"Good morning ladies. Please be seated. Have you eaten?"

They nodded yes and sat down.

Aka'r offered them some of the hot apple drink. Andromeda accepted graciously while Tama'r declined. Andromeda seemed a little dismayed by this. She was taught that if the King offers you something you take it. It doesn't matter if you like it or not.

Tama'r on the other hand met Aka'r enough times to realize that he did not expect blind obedience. He didn't even want to be king. He was a very wise man and a fit choice for ruler.

Tama'r said to the cook, "I'd like a cup of qahwah please."

He handed her the steaming cup of black liquid.

After the women had relaxed a bit Aka'r told them about the Demon. Their faces paled slightly and deep frowns creased their faces but they maintained their composure well.

Aka'r went on to explain about Shielka, the Staff and finally the Orb.

The women were in shock. The Orb had been a part of their history for centuries. The cornerstone of their very existence. Controlled rage contorted their features.

Aka'r explained that he did not feel Shielka came there to steal the Orb.

"It is more likely that when she came into contact with the Orb it stole her. Nevertheless, Shielka is very powerful. She uses a magic that is different than ours but equally as strong, if not stronger. We need to gain her trust so that she willingly returns the Orb to us."

When everything had been fully explained, Aka'r stood up and said, "Lets get started."

Relenting to the protests of his advisors, Aka'r agreed to allow two guards to accompany them.

Aka'r insisted that if any were to accompany him it would be Iron Fist and Sure Shot.

Iron Fist was a seasoned veteran. A short, stocky man of heavy build. He fought in many battles against the Orcs. A large double-bladed battle axe was set in a strap at his waist. The blade had numerous runes etched into it. He also walked with a short silver spear in his hand.

"For good luck," he would say.

Sure Shot was also a veteran of the Orc Wars. He carried a short bow in his hand as if it were a cane. There was no quiver of arrows on his back. And the bow was warped and appeared useless. It didn't even have a string, although it did have some curious runes etched into it. He also carried a short sword at his waist.

"Sure Shot must have been a great archer at one time to have earned that name. But since he carried a broken bow now he must just use the sword," thought Andromeda. She felt sorry for him.

After all of the introductions had been made they started off down the hill. They walked two abreast.

Fal'r insisted once again to carry the Staff of Oralin. He was in front and to the left of Iron Fist. Next in line were Aka'r and Tama'r. After them came Sure Shot and Andromeda.

When they reached the bottom of the hill the four guards in the crater greeted them.

Fal'r was shocked to see the size of the hole the staff had made. He was amazed that he was still alive and gripped the staff tightly.

Aka'r nodded at Fal'r and Fal'r spoke the name, "Shielka."

The staff immediately sprang up and moved around to point in a South Westerly direction.

Aka'r told Tama'r to send out her vision along the path the staff made.

Tama'r cast the appropriate spell and went into a slight trance.

After a few moments she said, "I don't see anything but scrub trees, brush and rabbits."

Aka'r responded, "Ready yourselves and lets be off."

At Aka'r's command Fal'r began walking forward with the staff out before him.

CHAPTER 19: THE DRUIDS

Hawthorne looked down upon Willow's body with a great sadness in his eyes. His shoulders drooped slightly and his mood was somber. He had sent Willow to her death, and that knowledge weighed heavily upon him.

After several minutes of silence, Hawthorne finally spoke to the crowd, "Willow has completed this cycle of her life. So it was in the beginning, so it is at the end. The wheel turns. We thank Willow for alerting us to the presence of Demons, once more roaming freely in our land. We honor her memory."

All of the Druids that were not on Guard duty were present, as were a few select members of Willow's village. Menja was there but he was still in shock and just stared straight ahead. His two best friends were helping him to move about, as he was unaware of his surroundings.

As Hawthorne slowly walked away from Willow's grave he mumbled softly to himself, "I should have known... I, above all others here, should have recognized the truly unnatural character of that storm."

"It's not your fault," came a soft voice from behind him.

Hawthorne turned around to see Sparrow, she had been Willow's best friend.

He spoke to her slowly and said, "I sent her to her death. It was by my word and my word alone that sent her to the Village of Tah. With her abilities she could have risen to the rank of Great Druid. She could have helped millions of living things all over the world. If it wasn't for my carelessness she would still be alive..."

"Willow would have gone to help her village even if you hadn't sent her. Wait, please let me finish. Willow had been talking about her village and home for many weeks.

She wanted to go back to prove to her father that she had made the right decision in coming here. Don't look so startled, all of us have had the same thoughts at one time or another. But for Willow it was much harder as Tah was so close. As for the Demons... How could you have known? They have not been seen here for centuries."

Hawthorne looked down at Sparrow and shook his head slowly. She had been like an older sister to Willow. Teaching Willow the ways of the Druids and helping her hone the edge of her skills. "So now you are council to an Elder?" he asked.

Sparrow looked at him then turned away, lowering her head she replied, "No Sir... I was just... I want to go after the Demons, I want to go after the Demons that killed her. I do not wish to fight them as I have no powers for that. But maybe I can follow them and learn their plans. If I have understood the legends correctly they are either moving toward or away from Cloud Mountain."

Hawthorne was amazed by what he was hearing. Here was a young woman, wanting to go out and fight Demons.

"Absolutely not", he replied, "You are confined to this grove until we find out what is going on and I judge it to be safe."

Sparrow watched in dismay as he turned and walked away from her.

"I must disobey him", she thought.

Her mind reeling under the pressure of that decision. Disobeying Hawthorne could mean immediate banishment from the Druid Society. She turned and walked slowly back to her niche in the Great Tree. She and Willow had shared this room. It used to feel so cramped, but now it felt big and empty.

As Sparrow gathered Willow's meager belongings to give to Menja, she picked up the chipped, dull sickle that was found next to Willow's body. Sparrow knew immediately that it wasn't Willow's. Willow prized her Golden Sickle more then any other of her possessions.

"The Demon must have taken Willow's and left this," she said through clinched teeth.

Slowly a smile came to her lips, a crooked, evil smile. Intense hatred built up inside of her and the desire to kill was overpowering.

Hawthorne was just coming up to Sparrow's room when he heard her scream. As he entered the room he saw Sparrow's face contorted and twitching, madness clearly shown through her eyes.

He yelled, "Sparrow... Sparrow stop."

Things seemed to move in slow motion then as Hawthorne watched in disbelief as Sparrow raised the sickle up in her right hand to kill him. Then as her arm swung down she lurched to one side and hurled the sickle into her straw bed. As soon as she was free of the sickle her body relaxed and she collapsed onto the floor.

Hawthorne called for help and knelt by Sparrow's side. His mind raced to find answers to what had just happened. Sparrow turned her head slightly and words formed on her lips.

"Evil," she mouthed, "So evil... I'm sorry."

Then her head rolled back limply and she was unconscious.

When others arrived, Hawthorne let them take Sparrow away to let her rest and help her if possible. Hawthorne stared at the sickle, now impaled in the bed.

He wasn't a Cleric but the Evil and anti-life emanations from the sickle were so powerful that even he could detect their presence.

"Why did they leave this? Did they plant it to grow hatred and needless destruction? We are a neutral people that seek a balance between good and evil. One cannot be allowed to dominate the other."

When Sparrow awoke she remembered what she had done and she felt ashamed. Now more then ever she was determined to find the Demons. She must help rid the world of them for Willow's memory and for her own sanity.

She worked on her plan in secret, planning the actions that would hopefully keep her safe, see the Demons dead and see Willow avenged.

Over the next few days she stashed away bits of food and travelling gear so that the quantities wouldn't be missed. Finally, it was time for her to act.

That night, using her Druid powers, Sparrow let her body merge into the Great Tree and traveled through its fiber to return to her old room. Once there she gathered the food and clothing and strapped on her sword belt. Sparrow never liked fighting but she was the undisputed master of the Scimitar. When she wielded it, she was able to move in such fluid motion the sword practically merged into part of her arm. She always seemed to know just what her opponent was going to do next.

When she had finished gathering her things she merged again with the Great Tree. This time she traveled down through the trunk into the life force of the ground itself. There was an ancient Oak tree in Tah and that is where she traveled to. When she reached the majestic Oak, she entered it through its roots and then moved up into its trunk. The powers that let her travel this way did not allow her to see out of the tree, only travel through it. Sparrow was quite unprepared for what she saw upon stepping out of the ancient Oak and into the village of Tah.

***

In his council chamber, Hawthorne was pacing back and forth. His advisors were watching him carefully all wondering what he would do. They had been alerted to Sparrow's departure by one of the caretakers noticing she was gone. Hawthorne knew where she went but he was uncertain if he should tell the others. If Sparrow succeeded in helping to defeat the Demons then his Druid Grove would gain much stature in the Druid Council.

If she failed and brought shame upon them he would be a laughing stock.

Hawthorne finally spoke, "After careful consideration I have decided not to take action against Sparrow. With the death of Willow, and Sparrow's possession by the Demon sickle, she cannot be expected to act rationally. I will give her some time to gather her thoughts and then we will see if further action is required."

Most in the chamber were relieved to hear this but Hemlock's face twisted and turned red. His eyebrows formed a deep 'V' in the center of his forehead.

Haltingly he said, "The rules of conduct are clear, Sparrow must be cast out and banished from Druid society forever, that is the law."

The room erupted in a fury of voices and Hawthorne commanded all to silence.

Staring at Hemlock he replied, "I am in charge here and my word is the law. I say no action is to be taken against Sparrow at this time. Do not try and undermine me again Hemlock."

Hawthorne's voice was acidic and it left no doubt to those present how he felt about Hemlock.

CHAPTER 20: THE TRANSFORMATION

As the Dragon's body diminished in size Talos's green eyes grew wider and wider. The dragon was slowly taking on the form of an Elf, an Elf that Talos knew. Talos just stared as Bedast took on the form of Ceylon. Ceylon was an Elf that occasionally visited Evergreen on his way to and from the holy city of Napaea.

When the transformation was completed Talos found his voice and spoke, "Why do you take on the form of Ceylon?"

"I 'am' Ceylon," the Dragon in Elf form replied.

Talos was uncertain as to what he should do next. He thought, "The knowledge that Dragons can change their shape and form has been rumored for centuries but never has there been any proof. But this can't be Ceylon, is sounds like him, but it can't be, Ceylon is an Elf."

Yet, the form that stood before him looked like an Elf, sounded like an Elf and moved like an Elf. Talos was worried.

Talos said, "If you are Ceylon then what did Queen Alia feast on during your last visit to Evergreen?"

Ceylon responded, "She feasted on the Red Fish from the Great Pond."

That answer did not make Talos very happy, it was the correct answer. His mind kept going over all of the times that he had met Ceylon, trying to remember any trait or flaw that might reveal this Dragon as an imposter. He could think of none. Ceylon had always been nondescript, coming into the city and just blending into the crowd. Talos remembered him only because it was his duty to remember all that entered Evergreen.

Even though he was only one half Elf, Talos had climbed the ranks to become the Captain of Queen Alia's Royal Guard.

"Ask me another," Ceylon said.

"No, I do not think so Bedast," Talos replied.

"I am in Elven form now, call me Ceylon" the Dragon said.

Shielka began to stir in Talos's arms. His arms were stiff from holding her for so long.

Ceylon said to Talos, "Do not tell her that I am Bedast. For now it is better for her mind not to know the truth. We will continue our discussion another time."

Talos nodded his head in agreement. "For now I'll play it your way," he thought, "but when Shielka is well and we're free of the Demons, then it will be my turn."

Shielka slowly opened her turquoise eyes and looked up to see Talos staring down at her. His face looked long and his eyes tired. His shoulders were drooping slightly as he held her in his arms.

"Lie still. You have not yet healed from your battle with the Orb," Talos said to Shielka.

Shielka looked up at Talos and said nothing. She was tired and sore and aching all over. She just wanted to curl up into a ball and go to sleep, but it hurt too much to move. Closing her eyes again Shielka began the relaxation exercises that she had learned throughout her Seer training. Slowly her mind relaxed and she began the slow tedious process of healing the wounds of her body and soul.

Ceylon watched Shielka's eyes open and close, and also watched Talos's reaction to her.

"Talos cares for this human," Ceylon thought, "He cares far more then he would like to admit, even to himself."

After living for centuries among Humans, Elves, Dwarves and their kind, Dragons understood the reading of emotions and signs, that others, too often, fail to see.

Ceylon walked up the hill to where Shielka and Talos had been when they first spotted him. When he reached the top he looked around and found Shielka and Talos's traveling gear. Talos's bow was also there. Ceylon picked everything up except the bow and walked back down the hill. When he reached Talos, Ceylon motioned for him to lift Shielka's head up a little higher so that he could place one of the packs under her head for a pillow.

After following Ceylon's instructions, Talos gently moved away from Shielka's still form.

"Get some rest Talos," Ceylon said.

"In a little while," Talos responded as he began walking up the hill.

The trip up was painful and he felt every jagged rock and clump of grass through his boots. When he reached the top he picked up his bow and examined it. He was surprised to see that Ceylon hadn't damaged it.

"That's odd," Talos thought, "Why didn't Ceylon destroy this when he had the chance? He knows that I carry magic arrows."

Turning back down the hill Talos watched Ceylon building a small smokeless fire near where Shielka rested.

Talos walked slowly and carefully down the hill and thought, "I must be going crazy, Ceylon is a Dragon, he need not fear my arrows, magic or not. By the time I got one off I would be nothing but a lump of charred flesh.

He is helping us, Shielka, because he himself has something to gain. Dragon's are evil, cunning and selfish beasts that do nothing but further their own ends. I will have to be very careful, if we are to survive to fight the Demons."

Talos reached the bottom of the hill and walked to where Ceylon had built the fire. The fire was perfect, no smoke or waste of fuel, it was compact and yet gave out a substantial amount of heat. He sat down next to it and felt its warmth against his bruised flesh and bone, and promptly fell asleep. Night had come to the small camp when Talos next opened his eyes. He was startled to find that he had fallen asleep and especially annoyed to find that a pillow had been placed under his head as well. He rolled over onto his knees and stood up. Shielka was still sleeping near the fire and Ceylon was roasting a small rabbit over the flames.

"I would have thought that a Dragon would prefer raw meat," Talos said.

"I do not have the gift of fire for no reason," Ceylon responded.

"Tell me more of your ability to change into Elf form," Talos said.

Ceylon turned to face Talos and fire clearly shown in the Dragons' eyes as he said, "Do not give me orders, Elf. I have allowed you to live as payment of a debt to the human girl. I promised not to harm her, not you. Choose your words carefully when addressing me."

Beads of sweat broke out on Talos' forehead as the weight of the Dragons' words sank in.

Talos responded, "I meant no disrespect Ceylon, please allow me to rephrase my question. Would you please tell me more of your ability to change into Elf form?"

"That is better," Ceylon said. Then he continued, "Your ancient Lore is filled with tales of Dragons having the ability to change form. What more can I tell?

Until now you have not believed the wisdom of the ancients. You have not believed the word of your ancestors. You only believed when you witnessed it for yourself. What can I say to someone with no faith in the past?

My life spans many generations and yours only spans one. What knowledge can you gain in your few years that I haven't already gathered in mine? You waste your youth making the mistakes of the past instead of learning and avoiding them by using the experience of others. Learn from the past, Talos of Evergreen, there you will find the answers you seek."

Talos was about to respond when he heard the now familiar sound of leathery wings flapping in the distance. Ceylon heard them to and quickly threw dirt onto the fire extinguishing it. The Demons had found them again.

CHAPTER 21: GARNATH ARRIVES

Garnath steps into the Multi-Dimensional Door on the Demon World and steps out onto a white sandy beach. The sun is low on the horizon and is slowly setting beneath the waves. Mellock and Likka step through next and are followed by six Lesser Demons. Garnath surveys the surroundings and a crooked smile plays upon his lips.

"Very good Mellock. You have chosen our entry point well."

"Thank you Lord Garnath."

Likka accentuates each and every step she takes. Her long smooth legs slowly and sensually carry her down toward the waters edge. All conversations stop cold and heads turn to watch her walk away. Cool evening waves caress her ankles as the tide slowly rolls out. None of the Demons want to miss a single detail of her seductive movements.

She stands in the cool water and stares out across the waves, her ebony eyes scanning the horizon.

"Where is the bitch Queen's island?", she asks.

Garnath glances at Mellock and then the other demons, and thinks, "Likka has such a wonderfully mesmerizing effect. They forget so quickly that she is a Succubus."

Mellock and the others stand silent and unmoving, they just stare at the richness of Likka's beauty.

"Mellock!" Garnath yells.

"Wha...?!? I'm sorry Lord Garnath, I was just..., did you say something?"

"Likka asked you a question Mellock and I strongly suggest that you do not keep her waiting for an answer.

Tell her where the Queen's Island is, now."

"Yes Lord Garnath. The Queen's island is over in that direction."

Likka turns away from the water and looks back toward Mellock to see which direction he's pointing. Her full sensuous lips glisten in the dim light of sunset and she mouths the words 'thank you' and blows Mellock a kiss. She arches her back slightly, stretches her lean body and turns toward the horizon trying to get a glimpse of the Queen's island.

Mellock keeps pointing with his left hand, his human hand. His immense right arm, which could uproot a tree, hangs limply as he scratches his right ankle. He just stands there watching her. His head and eyes following her every movement, his left arm still outstretched toward the horizon.

Garnath leans over and slaps Mellock across the back of the head.

"Wake up Mellock. The rest of you idiots wake up."

Garnath had no patience for Demons that lacked intelligence. He had commands for them yes, but patience, no.

"Mellock, where is that little Imp of yours?"

Mellock rubs the back of his head and says, "Firefly? He should be here any minute Lord Garnath."

As if on que the small Imp comes skipping over the treetops and lands on the beach near Likka. She looks down and smiles at him, her long white fangs sparkling in the moonlight. Firefly blushes and turns away from her.

"Firefly come here," said Mellock.

Firefly snatched another brief look at Likka and quickly hopped over to where Mellock stood.

"Give us your report Imp."

"Going in 'Z' pattern toward middle of land. See small camp fire. Scout flew down to see. Surprised by Talos. They fight. I go behind Talos to kill him. Energy bolt shot at me. Very small, not hurt. I see human girl. I go attack her. She turns into Goddess. Lightning all around, and pain, such pain. Emptiness. Emptiness like stuck in Dimension Door forever."

Firefly begins shaking. He falls to the ground and holds himself in a tight ball and whimpers.

What had been a routine though unusual report immediately commanded their attention with the word Goddess. Garnath walks over to Firefly and kicks him.

"Get up Imp, Get up."

The Imp rolled along the ground and cried out, "Banish me. Send me away. Send home. Such pain. Such Pain. I remember. I remember. Banish me from here. Banish me."

Garnath and the other demons jumped away from the Imp. To be banished was the worst punishment that could be cursed upon Demonkind.

Likka walks over to Garnath and says, "A demon asking to be banished, impossible. Unless... he really did see a Goddess."

Likka knelt down beside Firefly and cradled him in her arms.

"It's alright now Firefly, you're safe with me. I'll protect you."

Firefly looked up into Likka's molten ebony eyes and was lost. The Demons watched the Imp visibly relax in her arms.

Likka's voice was enchanting and she said, "I want to help you Firefly. But you need to help me to help you. Tell me more about what you saw when Scout fought Talos. Leave out no detail. Then, I will make your every dream come true."

Firefly's muscles tensed for a moment but then relaxed again.

"Flying 'Z' toward Fire Mountain. Scout saw camp fire. Confused. Could not find people. They are there. Cannot find. Scout go to land. Talos attack from behind with sword. I land behind Talos. Go to attack from behind. Energy bolt hit me. Made hole in ground. Talos blinded. Stupid humans. Scout jump on Talos tear his body. I see human girl. I go to attack her. She screams. She put arms up. Lightning around her. Lightening arms, legs, head. Explosion in my body. Emptiness. Pain. Emptiness. I run away. Scout turn white, yellow, white explode. I run. Call Garnath. I come here."

Likka had been rubbing the bony ridges between the Imp's wings to help keep him calm during his report.

She continues to rub his back and says, "Tell me more about the girl. Describe her."

"Human. Short. Fire hair. Snake skin. Goddess."

Likka curled her lips into a grimace when the Imp said, "Goddess."

"I don't understand 'Snake Skin', what do you mean by that?"

"Snake skin. Body. Maybe her body snake. Maybe cover. Maybe not. I run. Goddess. Drain life. I run."

"Sleep now Firefly, sleep and dream."

111

Firefly quit moving while Likka continued to stroke the ridges of his back. When Firefly had fallen asleep she bent down and whispered into his ear. A smile came to his crooked face as her enchantments made him dream of them in a blissful, romantic embrace. After casting her spell she moved away from him and Firefly lay back on the sandy beach and slept.

Likka walks over to Garnath and says, "A human female body with snake skin, that can drain life energy and use magic. Some kind of Greater Demon / Succubus half-breed?"

"No. I don't think so."

"What about an Undead?" Likka asked.

"Talos in league with the Undead? Or even a Demon or Demon cross-breed? I think not. Perhaps she was disguised and the Imp was too frightened to take notice. Or perhaps, just perhaps, Talos has been able to enslave a Demigod. A Demigod would have the powers that the Imp has described."

"A Demigod! How are we supposed to fight a Demigod?"

"We do not have to fight her, we have to free her. Only a Goddess of Evil would use the power to drain life energy against an enemy. The 'Good Goddesses' use love and happiness to combat their enemies, not obliteration. Talos must have some power or spell over her and she is obligated to protect him. That must be it. Why else has it been so hard for Demonkind to track him down? How else could a Demon be totally destroyed? He must have something that has power over her: a ring, a gem, an amulet... Her soul."

Likka and the others drew back in horror. The words, "Her soul" echoed in their minds.

"Yes, that is the only way that a goddess would submit. He has trapped her soul and is forcing her to do his bidding. Yet, that is not the way Talos usually acts. I have had many reports on this Half-Elf, he has powers of his own. To enslave someone goes against the nature of the reports I have on him."

Garnath spins around and looks down at Likka.

"What do you mean, you have reports on him? Since when do you command?"

Garnath reaches out, grabs Likka by the throat and lifts her off of the ground.

"Tell me what you have learned. Now!" Garnath commanded.

Likka realized her slip of the tongue too late and tried to recover her mistake.

"I... I can't breath... I did it for you my Lord... You were busy... I tried to help you... I can't breath..."

Garnath released his grip and let her drop to the ground.

The force of Garnath's words drove the other Demons back and one of them stepped on Firefly. The sudden jolt brought Firefly out of his trance. Firefly became conscious very reluctantly and very slowly. To his mind the romantic interlude with Likka had been real and he resented the intrusion. As he became fully aware of what was going on around him Firefly became deathly still. He watched in horror as Garnath first choked Likka and then dropped her. Likka looked a little bruised but she was still alive.

"Not kill Garnath now. Kill when Garnath weak. Kill Garnath. Save Likka. Kill Garnath," thought Firefly.

"Speak!"

Likka looked down at Garnath's clawed feet and said, "I was only trying to please you Lord Garnath. I had heard of Talos and since you were busy I thought that you would be pleased with me. I only sought to please you Lord Garnath. All I ever want to do is please you."

"Enough of this petty drivel. Speak to me of Talos."

Firefly watched on in silent fury as Garnath continued to humiliate Likka.

"Kill Garnath. Kill Garnath." He thought over and over again.

"Talos is from the great Elven city of Evergreen where he is the Captain of the Royal Guard. He is one of the most skilled Elven swordsmen in the world and he fights with an ancient, enchanted blade.

No one has ever seen him call upon the blade's powers in battle and it's powers remain a mystery. Talos has some spell casting ability but something about his nature limits his ability to use it. He also carries many magical devices of mundane nature and none of no great importance."

"What is his current mission?"

"The information is vague Lord Garnath but most agree on one point. He is searching for the Kingdom of Cepheus. He hopes to ally the Elves with them prior to entering into battle against us."

"The Kingdom of Cepheus... We must stop him and free the Goddess before Talos makes contact with them. Imp! Take us to where you saw Talos and the Goddess."

Firefly burned with the desire to strike out and kill Garnath.

"When weak. I kill." Firefly thought, "When weak. I kill."

Firefly steps toward Likka and extends his small hand to help her up. Garnath lashes out with a foot and kicks

Firefly's hand away nearly breaking it. Firefly rolls back and takes up a fighting stance.

Likka looks at Firefly and says, "I'm alright, just show Lord Garnath the way."

Garnath kicks Likka and sends her sprawling across the sand as well.

"Now Imp! Show us the way."

Firefly takes another quick look at Likka and nods. He begins flying inland and Garnath signals the others to follow.

Fireflies thoughts are of Garnath, "Kill Garnath. "Kill Garnath..."

CHAPTER 22: OOPS

Fal'r gripped the staff tightly and walked along in front of the small band. He held the staff out before him like a knight with a lance.

They traveled like this with Fal'r being guided by the staff for many days traversing mostly low hills, with sparse brush and thin trees.

Iron Fist tried to stay way out in front of Fal'r to ensure the path was clear. It was tiring work as he had to keep looking back to ensure that he was in fact going in the right direction.

Sure Shot kept a position mid way between Iron Fist and Fal'r.

But now they were heading into areas where the trees were larger and there were more of them. Fal'r had to continually maneuver around them and the thick underbrush.

This forced Iron Fist and Sure Shot to close the gap and be nearly on top of Fal'r and so could no longer scout ahead for anything laying in wait.

And then they came upon their first major obstacle. The staff did not follow the old animal trail that headed roughly south-southwest. The staff pulled Fal'r directly southwest toward a gigantic boulder. Fal'r tried to steer the staff back toward the path to avoid being smashed into the huge rock but the staff would not deviate from its selected course.

Instead of telling the staff to stop, Fal'r quickly cast a flying spell.

Fal'r gracefully took off into the morning sky and sailed over the boulder that moments before had blocked his path.

The other members of the small band quickly took the less direct route and ran around the boulder.

"Fal'r slow down," Aka'r yelled.

But Fal'r kept pulling away from the small band, flying further and further toward the southwest.

Fal'r was having trouble controlling the staff and his Flying spell at the same time. While on the ground Fal'r was able to keep the pace slow and easy by offering resistance to the staff with his feet. But now he was flying and unable to offer the same control.

"Time to go down," Fal'r thought.

"Land," he said.

Nothing happened.

Fal'r kept flying faster and faster toward the southwest.

"Land", he said giving the command once more.

Still nothing.

"The staff must be in control of the fly spell," he thought.

"Aka'r... Aka'r... Help!"

Aka'r said to the small band, "Keep up as best you can. I'm going to fly after Fal'r. The staff must have taken control of his magic."

Aka'r then cast his own Fly spell and shot off into the air after Fal'r.

Iron Fist said, "Well, you heard the man, let's get moving."

He started running down the path at a quick but measured pace.

The other members of the band began running after him. Tama'r had drifted to the rear of the group. Even though she was in good physical condition, the others, Andromeda included, had physical exercise as part of their daily routine. They were starting to distance themselves from her.

Tama'r called out, "Andromeda wait... Andromeda..."

Andromeda looked back and saw Tama'r slowing her pace and panting heavily.

Andromeda stopped running and called back to Tama'r, "Come on. We have to keep up with them."

Tama'r, breathing heavy, jogged up to Andromeda and grasped her shoulder for support.

"I can't keep up this pace."

"Just a minute then, let's rest a moment."

"Thank you."

Andromeda sat down and untied the top of her pack. She rummaged through it for a few moments then said, "Ah ha, I found it. I knew it was in here someplace."

"What is it?"

"This," Andromeda responded.

She held up a small blue vial with tiny figures drawn on it.

"What is it?"

"Well, look, silly," Andromeda said and handed the vial to Tama'r.

Tama'r took the vial and held it up to her face. Looking at it very closely she could see that the tiny pictures were of people exercising.

"I don't understand."

"I thought you were a Mage," said Andromeda playfully.

"I am a Mage. Well sort of a Mage. I never had much interest in fireballs and weather and lightning so I concentrated in Far-Seeing. But in order to make it through the ranks to become a full blooded certified Mage you have to master 'all' of the magic disciplines. I only mastered one."

Tama'r turned away from Andromeda and held her head downcast and did not look up.

She held the bottle out toward Andromeda and said, "Come on, lets go. I'm rested now."

"Just a minute, that's what I was trying to tell you. That potion will give you strength and vitality. You will be able to run and keep up with us, probably even run faster and further then Iron Fist himself."

Tama'r quickly forgot the pain of the last few moments and said, "What do I do?"

"You drink it silly."

Tama'r blushed and said, "Oh."

Tama'r then removed the wax stopper from the vial and looked into it. Inside the vial was a milky white colored substance that seemed to swirl around of its own accord. She sniffed it but didn't smell anything.

"What's it taste like?"

"Arg... Just drink it so we can get going. The others already have a big lead on us. Hurry up."

Tama'r held her nose, just in case, and drank the potion all in one shot.

"Hey, that tastes good."

119

"Will you come on?" said Andromeda as she began running down the path after the others.

Tama'r felt the potion tingle her insides as it traveled down her throat and into her stomach. It traveled quickly throughout her whole body.

"I feel wonderful," she said.

Seeing Andromeda already running away, Tama'r jumped up and began running after her.

"This is great," she thought, "So easy. I need to find out more about that potion."

Tama'r was able to catch up with Andromeda very easily and she ran past saying, "Catch me if you can."

Andromeda called after her, "Tama'r wait. We must not get separated. Tama'r..."

Tama'r laughed and stopped running. "Come on Andromeda, what are you waiting for?"

Andromeda caught up with her and they continued running together.

"I didn't think you were going to stop."

"It feels so good, I almost didn't. What was in that potion?"

"Magic," Andromeda replied with a wink.

They both laughed and continued running down the trail.

Aka'r had caught up with Fal'r and was trying to decide on a course of action.

"If you tell the staff to stop, what will happen?"

"I'll probably fall."

"You wouldn't be able to stop my fall with a spell because the staff would absorb it. How about altering the terrain beneath me to absorb the impact?"

"I could try a Control Plants spell and have the trees catch you?"

"That sounds like a good idea but do you think the Staff will allow the trees to catch me? Maybe it will move them out of the way."

"Hmmmmm... If you gave the command to stop, and then dropped the staff, I could stop your fall and then we could land and pick up the staff again."

"That sounds like the best plan so far," Fal'r said, "Ready?"

"Ready."

"Stop!" commanded Fal'r.

Abruptly he stopped in mid-air and began to fall. Quickly he released his hold on the staff and they both plummeted toward the ground below.

Aka'r said, "Feather Flight" and pointed toward Fal'r.

Fal'r immediately slowed and his fall became the gentle downward motion of a feather.

The Staff was not as fortunate and it picked up speed as it hurtled toward the ground. Iron Fist and Sure Shot were close enough to see what was happening and watched as the staff fell.

Iron Fist and Sure Shot were not the only ones watching the action in the sky. Darrow had been sent out ahead of Zak and Arnot to scout the area between them and Cloud Mountain. Darrow felt the power of the staff and had gone to investigate and he watched closely as the Staff now fell away from the puny humans.

Iron Fist grabbed Sure Shot by the arm and cried out, "Look!"

He pointed to Darrow's huge Demon form flying up through the trees and into the morning sky. They watched helplessly as Darrow's massive claws reached to pluck the staff out of the air, and they knew with the first touch, the Demon would gain the power of the ancients.

CHAPTER 23: SPARROW

After Sparrow stepped out of the ancient Oak and into the village of Tah, her eyes went wide with revulsion at what she saw. The moon barely gave off enough light and what she saw was shocking. The village was all but leveled and the few buildings that were still standing had gaping holes torn in them. There were a few men walking around and she approached one of them.

"Excuse me. Excuse me."

"Begone from the accursed place woman," he said.

"What happened here?"

The man drew back in shock and said, "You do not know? Everyone within a hundred miles knows what happened here. Your cloths are strange, and dry, but it was raining earlier. Who are you and where are you from?"

Sparrow watched the man's eyes as they studied her. His eyes held for an instant on her Scimitar within its sheath.

"I am a Druid."

The man took a step backwards and said, "You have brought this upon us. You brought the Demons and they destroyed our village. It's your fault my family is dead, your fault."

He clinched his fist into a ball and swung at Sparrow and yelled, "I've got one... I've captured a Demon..."

Sparrow ducked under the man's swing and kicked him in the groin. She heard the heavy footsteps of people running toward her so she turned and ran down one of the village side streets. In the shadows of the ruined buildings she felt reasonably sure that they couldn't find her.

She was breathing heavily and trying to move silently when she entered one of the buildings.

The building was half destroyed with the roof caving in, and yet there were fresh flowers in small vases resting in the center of the floor. Then she saw his still form in the darkness staring at her. She reached for her sword and stopped. The man was unmoving, as if a statue. It was Menja. Sparrow slowly walked to his side but he remained motionless, paralyzed with grief. He just stared straight ahead, at the spot where his daughter was slain.

"Menja," Sparrow whispered, "Menja."

No response.

"Menja, I am going after the demons that did this to Willow. I am going to make them... To make them pay for what they have done to her."

Sparrow sat with Menja in silence for a long time.

Finally she said, "She loved you Menja. She wanted to come home but... Her place was with us. She accepted that, and although there were many times that she wanted to leave and return home, she couldn't. Willow said that you had always taught her to help others. She said that she could best serve those around her by using her special gift to reach out and help everyone. She wanted you to be proud of her, she couldn't quit and go home. She felt that she would have betrayed all that you taught her. Just remember that she loved you."

Sparrow stood up and walked away from Menja. She listened carefully for sounds of other villagers but heard nothing. As she stepped back out through the opening in the wall, she looked back and saw Menja crying and tears formed in her eyes as well.

She softly whispered, "Grieve Menja, grieve and you will heal."

Sparrow walked carefully down the side street and ran toward the nearby river. Along the waters edge were many trees and bushes that she might be able to gather information from. She positioned herself so that she could watch the village and be close to an old Weeping Willow tree at the same time. She held up her arms and began the enchantments that would allow her to communicate with the great tree.

"Weeping Willow hear my plea, come to life and speak with me. Weeping Willow hear my plea, come to life and speak with me," she chanted.

The tree gave a mighty shrug and said, "Who calls to me?"

"Greetings Great Willow, it is I, Sparrow of the Druids. I need to know about the Demons, the ones that destroyed this village."

The tree replied, "Three flew down the river and then the rains came. Two returned and destroyed the village."

"What did they look like and did you see them leave with a Golden Sickle?"

"One was large, the other small. The small one held a Golden Sickle when he left."

"Which way did they go?"

The tree drew back some of its branches and extended others to point in an easterly direction, slightly away from the direct path of the river.

"Thank you Great Willow."

"You are welcome."

Sparrow walked along the waters edge and followed it downstream. She could hear the villagers shouts and they did not sound happy.

She was certain that they were looking for her and she did not want to be found.

When she was well past the village she stopped to talk to a small patch of blackberry bushes. They told her that Demons had flown down stream but they never saw any fly back. She thanked them and continued on her way. She repeated this line of questioning several times with various plants along the way until she found one that had not seen anything at all. She knew from what the Weeping Willow had told her that the Demons had traveled on this side of the river. She crawled up over the embankment and walked a short way inland and tried to pick up the trail again.

The sun was just beginning to rise when Sparrow came to a rocky outcropping with a cave dug into it. It had an unusually large opening. She could tell by huge claw marks and the sharp edges that it had been made recently. She entered the cave and was hit by a pungent odor. It stung her nose and made her eyes water. Quickly she ran out and away from the cave entrance. As her eyes cleared and the sun came up a little higher in the morning sky, Sparrow could make out the hulking mass of a half eaten cow in the hollow cavern.

"This must be the right direction."

She walked over to a nearby tree and once again cast the spell that allowed her to talk to plants. She asked it which way the Demons had gone and the tree pointed to the southeast. She thanked it and began a slow jog in that direction. After running for some time Sparrow stopped and ate some of the fruit and berries that she had been carrying.

She was tired and decided to rest for a few moments.

She closed hers eyes for what she thought would be but a few moments.

Hours later she suddenly awoke. She knew she was being watched. She looked around quickly then laughed.

Nearby was a small Unicorn Rabbit watching her intently. Sparrow tossed some blackberries at it and watched as the rabbit jumped away and then returned. It approached the berries cautiously and sniffed them. Almost at once it began eating the sweet berries of the river.

Sparrow enjoyed watching the animals and it gave her some peace from the hectic pace of her quest. After resting a little while longer, Sparrow began her slow run once again toward the east. The Unicorn Rabbit ran a few paces behind Sparrow waiting for her to drop more of the succulent berries.

Sparrow tried to shoo the rabbit away but it just kept following her. It wasn't so much that the rabbit bothered her as she ran, but she was afraid that when she slowed down she'd be skewered by the two foot horn that crowned the rabbit's forehead.

When it was time to rest again Sparrow stepped behind a tree so that if the rabbit didn't stop in time it would stab the tree and not her. Sure enough she felt the tree shake and heard the thud of the rabbit's horn hit the tree.

Sparrow stepped out from behind the tree and looked down at a comical sight. The rabbit was stuck to the tree.

She reached down and speaking softly to the rabbit, helped it to free itself. She examined the wound in the tree and saw that it was bleeding. She knelt down and put some healing herbs over the wound and tied them loosely around the trunk with some old vines.

She rested near the tree and sang softly to it as she fed the rabbit more of the berries. She sang about her home and her life with the Druids.

She was lonely and wanted to go back, but knew that she couldn't, not until she found the Demons.

She started running again.

After traveling all day like this it was time to make camp for the night. The rabbit was still with her so she decided to ask it its name.

After casting her spell to speak with animals Sparrow said, "What is your name rabbit?"

"Promise not to laugh and I'll tell."

Sparrow was surprised by that response as she had never had an animal show this kind of intelligence before, to be embarrassed about their name.

"My name is Sparrow and I promise that I will not laugh."

"My name is Spike," the rabbit replied as it swung its head back and forth.

"Spike. That is a wonderful name."

"You like it?"

"Of course, Why shouldn't I?"

"My friends make fun of me. They say it's a silly name. We all have spikes on our head so why be called spike?"

"That is why it is such a wonderful name. It is a good description of what you are. My name is Sparrow but do I look like a bird?"

She twirled around once in front of Spike.

"Hey, you're right, I never thought of that. Spike, it is a good name, a great name, thank you Sparrow. Thank you for the berries, I was very hungry."

"I need to make camp now and get some sleep. You can stay here if you like."

"I have slept here before, you have found a nice place to sleep."

"Did you see the Demons come through here."

Spike shrank back and said, "Yes. They were very bad."

"Which way did they go from here?"

"They were a days journey that way," said Spike pointing toward the southeast.

"Are you sure they are still there?"

"No, but I smelled them at sunrise and it was very strong."

"Will you take me to them?"

"Will you give me more berries?"

"Yes, of course," said Sparrow, and she threw another handful of berries to the fat rabbit.

"Thank you, I will show you the way tomorrow."

Sparrow slept on the hard ground while Spike stood guard over her. Being usually counted as prey, he was a very light sleeper anyway.

They started out in the morning after a healthy breakfast of fruit and berries. The rabbit led the way this time and Sparrow was glad not to have that horn nipping at her behind.

Morning turned into afternoon and Spike stopped in his tracks.

"Demons here, walking."

Sparrow examined the ground and saw that there were three sets of distinct clawprints in the dirt. Two of the sets headed along to the left while the largest pair headed off to the right. Sparrow elected to go to the right as she would rather confront only one Demon at a time.

She traveled for what seemed like days and saw an unusual sight in the sky almost directly above her. There were two men flying toward the southwest. Suddenly one stopped in mid flight and the other flew past him.

"They must be fighting," she thought.

Then the first man dropped his staff and began plummeting toward the earth. The second man waved his arms and pointed at the first man and his fall slowed to a gradual descent.

She then saw the huge form of a massive Demon flying up into the sky to attack the men. But instead of flying toward the men it flew toward the staff. She heard the men's screams as they saw the Demon flying toward the staff and she wondered what it meant.

CHAPTER 24: THE GODDESS

Firefly half flew, half hopped along the tops of the trees. Looking back he saw Likka and the others flying closely behind him. Garnath was first, followed by Mellock and Likka. The lesser Demons were lagging a little further back. Firefly grinned an Impish grin and began moving a little faster along the treetops.

Garnath and Mellock were absorbed in a discussion of the finer art of torture and how it would apply to Talos. Likka spread her wings and soared up and down, right and left. Her wings hardly moved as she rode the thermal currents of the sky. The six Lesser Demons were falling further and further behind. While they were strong and did have wings of sorts, they could not keep up with the ever increasing pace being set by the Imp.

Firefly periodically looked back over his shoulder at the others. With the Lesser Demons still in sight he gradually changed course to the north and began moving faster once more. Soon the Lesser Demons were out of sight and he changed course back to the east.

Firefly thought, "Others gone. Imp smart. Little Demons stupid."

They flew without stopping to rest and Firefly's pace was starting to slow. Firefly spotted a small clearing and headed toward it.

Garnath noticed the abrupt change in course and slowly stopped his forward motion.

He called to Firefly, "Imp. Imp get back here."

Firefly continued down into the clearing and disappeared from Garnath's view.

Garnath clinched his clawed hands and turned toward Mellock.

131

"Get me that Imp."

Mellock flew down into the clearing after Firefly.

Garnath whirled around and looked behind them but saw only Likka staring at him. He flew up higher and higher but could see nothing. His face was contorted and his clawed hands shook violently as he descended into the clearing.

"Where are those idiot Demon guards of yours Mellock?"

Mellock had been talking with Firefly and called back to Garnath, "Lord Garnath, Firefly says that he looked back and no longer saw the others. He stopped here so that we could rest and wait for them."

Firefly hid behind Mellock and did not look directly at Garnath. Firefly was panting heavily from the exertion of the pace that he had set.

Garnath looked down at the Imp in disgust.

"You pitiful creature," Garnath said, "Very well, we rest here and wait for the others."

"Likka, find us some food."

Likka's eyebrows dug deep furrows into her forehead as she heard Garnath's command. She raised her arm and pointed toward Mellock and was about to speak when Garnath stepped toward her.

"I said, get us some food... Now."

Likka sprang back away from Garnath. Likka was amazed at the difference in Garnath since leaving the Demon World. There, he would never have treated her this way. He was mad for power but not mad. Likka backed further away from Garnath.

When she was out of his initial striking range she turned and headed for the forest to hunt.

The bony ridges on Firefly's back were stiff and upright. His tail was coiled and ready to strike. But Garnath was still too strong and so he held back.

Firefly wearily hopped after Likka and said, "I help Likka, I help Likka."

Likka turned to see Garnath kicking at the Imp and missing as Firefly hopped past him.

Likka looked down into Firefly's eyes and saw what burned there.

She thought, "This little Imp would do battle with Garnath if I wanted him to. But then, so would any creature, given enough time to work on him."

She said, "Thank you Firefly. You go out ahead and find us some food, I'll follow you."

She reached down and patted Firefly on the head.

Firefly then briskly sprang into the trees, he kept sniffing the air trying to find the scent of an animal to hunt. It didn't take him long before he found one.

He called to Likka, "Animal smell."

Then he moved on into the trees.

Likka was following behind Firefly and carefully watched the area ahead for signs of the animal. The first thing she noticed were it's tracks. Huge clawed feet that made deep impressions into the ground.

"A Demon?" No, Firefly had said an animal. Very strange, it walks on two legs and then on four."

Firefly's screams brought Likka out of her thoughts and back to the animal. She heard a loud crashing sound coming quickly toward her. Peering between the trees she saw Firefly inches ahead of a very large hairy beast. The beast was like none she had ever seen. Long black hair covering its entire body except for a long muzzle full of sharp teeth. It was a large fat animal running on all four feet. Its bulk was moving swiftly and gracefully after Firefly.

Firefly hopped toward Likka screaming, "Help! Help!"

Likka stepped out from behind the tree and directly into the creature's path. She unfolded her wings to their full 12 foot span, bared her long sharp fangs and hissed at the creature.

The bear instinctively panicked and tried to slow itself. It dug all 4 paws into the ground. But it was traveling too fast to stop and it lunged for Likka. Likka effortlessly flew a few feet into the air and the bear fell headlong onto the spot where she had just been. Quickly she dropped down upon the bear's back and slit its throat with her dagger. The bear fell lifeless to the ground.

Likka looked around for Firefly but could not see him.

She called out, "Firefly. Firefly come here."

Firefly came walking back toward her slowly. His head was downcast. His long spindly tail was coiled around his waist.

When he was closer he said, "Sorry. I run away. Sorry."

Before he could say any more Likka spoke up, "You were great! You had a very good plan little one. You found the animal and brought it back to me to kill it. Garnath said for me to bring back the food. If you would have killed it then we would both be in trouble. You did very well to bring the animal to me."

Firefly replied, "But..."

Likka cut him off by saying, "Come now Firefly, you did well. Now you must help me get this huge beast back to Garnath."

The bear was heavier than Likka believed possible. Try as they might, Likka and Firefly could barely move it.

"Firefly, go and get Mellock to help. If they want to eat, they can carry this beast back themselves."

Firefly smiled and flew off through the thin trees toward the camp. When he arrived he carefully avoided going near Garnath.

He approached Mellock and said, "Food. Big creature. Heavy. Need help. Heavy. Carry."

"Lord Garnath, apparently they have killed an animal but it is too large for them to pack. Should I go and help them?"

Garnath had been staring out toward the west, scanning the skies for the other Demons, but saw nothing.

"Yes, go. I'm growing impatient for something to eat."

Mellock started to leave and Garnath called after him, "Mellock."

"Yes Lord Garnath?"

"If it isn't here soon I'll have to eat your little Imp for dinner..."

"Yes Lord Garnath. But I shall return shortly and save you the discomfort of having to eat such a small meal as an Imp."

Firefly shuddered at the thought and scrambled out ahead of Mellock.

"Quickly. Quickly," Firefly said to Mellock.

When they reached Likka she had already eaten a small portion of the bear. Fresh blood trickled down from the side of her mouth.

Likka smiled seductively at Mellock as she said, "Would you like something to nibble on?"

Mellock smiled back but said nothing. He reached down and began to lift the bear. Its weight was unlike anything he had encountered on this world before. Still, he was not going let that stop him.

When they reached the camp, Garnath was still standing facing the west and looking up into the sky.

"Lord Garnath, here is your food. A powerful and mighty animal of this world, a bear."

He dropped the meat at Garnath's feet. He knew the error of not letting Garnath choose his meal first.

Garnath looked at the mass of flesh and fur at his feet.

"How large was this beast?"

Likka replied before Mellock could answer, "It was nothing Lord Garnath. A small beast really, only about as tall as my wings are wide. It was certainly no match for Demonkind."

Garnath again looked down at the massive limbs of the beast. It's arms and legs ended in huge claws and these were supported by enormous muscles. He tore off a leg and pointed for the others to eat as well. He studied Likka carefully, he never thought that she was capable of such a feat. He nodded his approval as he smiled at her.

Likka saw in Garnath's eyes a new found respect for her abilities. But she knew she must be careful and not appear to be a threat to him.

Likka returned Garnath's smile and nodded while she thought, "I will bide my time and when the moment is right, I will kill you."

CHAPTER 25: SURPRISED

Ceylon quickly threw dirt on the fire extinguishing it.

"Talos, wake Shielka, quickly."

Talos stepped over to Shielka's sleeping form and gently put his hand on her shoulder.

"Shielka," he said, "Shielka, wake up."

Shielka sat up quickly and then began to fall back down.

Talos grabbed her and said, "The Demons have returned."

Shielka shook her head very slowly from front to back and then rolled it back and forth between her shoulders. She turned toward Talos and grabbed for him in the darkness.

Talos asked, "What is wrong?"

"Nothing Talos, I will be fine in a moment."

Shielka closed her eyes and within her mind she willed the power to come forth and give her night vision. When she opened her eyes she once again saw the blood red outlines of Talos, the trees and then another Elf.

The image of this Elf was a blur. The intensity of his aura was almost blinding and Shielka had to turn away from him.

"Talos, they are almost upon us. Ready your sword and I'll ready my magic. Shielka should conserve her energy," said Ceylon.

Shielka said to Talos, "How does he know my name and who is he? Where is the Dragon?"

"Not now," Talos said.

The flapping of the Demon wings grew louder, as did the stench.

Zak asked Arnot, "Are you sure you spotted something over here?"

"Yes General."

Then Zak felt it. The unmistakable presence of magic. He scanned the ground below and spotted the three travelers and recognized Talos immediately.

"There they are. Two of them are masking my detection spell," he said while pointing toward them.

Zak called out to those on the ground below while Arnot continued on to land in the brush behind them, "Talos, I would speak with you."

Talos was startled by the Demons words but quickly recovered and said, "Begone Demon. I have nothing to say to you except leave or die."

Zak descended slowly to the fringe of the small camp. His glowing eyes caught sight of Shielka and he felt the power that emanated from her. He glanced at the other Elf and felt nothing.

"Talos, I am not attacking you and I know that your code of honor does not permit you to attack, only defend. You will hear my words."

Talos had his sword held out in front of him as he faced the Demon.

"Speak foul one."

"I am called Zak. You have caused much trouble Talos, and have become quite a curiosity among us. You recently fought one of my scouts and completely destroyed him.

You are well known for your absolute intolerance for Evil creatures and for some unknown reason an intolerance of Demons as well. So you can understand our delight to discover that you have done such an Evil act. To banish a Demon is one thing, but to so totally and completely destroy one is a truly Evil deed.

Our Queen, Balar, would like to discuss this with you. Your companions may also attend if you wish. My Queen resides on a lovely little Island that most of your kind would find pleasant. The inhabitants are very friendly and look very much like... your companion... the human girl..."

Talos's knuckles began to turn white as his hands gripped his sword tighter and tighter.

Talos was about to speak when Ceylon stepped forward and said, "Talos this Demon appears sincere and we could possibly benefit by cooperating with them. There is more than enough of this world that we could share."

"What?!?" said Talos.

"Talos my friend, we should discuss his offer."

Talos stepped back and said to Zak, "We will discuss your offer. Leave us and return tomorrow at first light."

"Very good Talos, I will return at that time to accept your agreement."

Zak extended his long wings and took off into the night sky.

Arnot caught up with him and said, "We should kill them."

"Balar wants Talos alive. We will kill the other two when we reach the island."

Arnot watched Zak fly ahead and said softly to himself, "We should kill them now."

Talos watched Zak fly away and also caught sight of the other Demon flying up to meet him. When he was sure that they were gone he wheeled about to face Ceylon and said, "Are you crazy?"

"If you were less caught up in your own anger you would have noticed him studying Shielka. He must not find out about the Orb. Also, Shielka is different from others that live here.

"Demons cannot know that by just looking at someone."

"Talos look at her. Her skin is darker, her clothing resembles snake skin but is actually tanned fish hides, she wears sandals instead of boots... Shall I go on? Their Queen it seems lives on a island, in the same place that Shielka is from, a coincidence?"

Talos looked at Shielka and stepped away from her.

"What do you know of this?"

Shielka's mouth opened and her eyes grew wide.

"I know nothing of this."

"You said that you come from an island. Their Queen lives on an island. The people there look like you... You destroyed the Demon that attacked us earlier? You didn't just banish it back to the Demon world?"

Tears formed in Shielka's eyes and she said, "I don't know what happened to it. My only thoughts were to save you. I didn't care how. But if their Queen is living on one of the remaining islands, then that is how my home was destroyed. All of my people were killed, my island home now lies deep beneath the ocean and I am the last of my tribe. I had hoped that the dreams were false and that I would someday find my way back home. But now I see the dreams were true. The terrible dreams were true."

141

Shielka put her head in her hands and began weeping.

"Talos this appears to be a great opportunity for you and Shielka," said Ceylon.

"What are you talking about?"

Ceylon gave a short chuckle and said, "You are being invited to speak with the Demon Queen. There will be no guards or armies to fight through. You will have an opportunity to kill her and throw the Demons into confusion. You will accomplish your mission of driving out the Demons and Shielka will have the satisfaction of avenging the deaths of her people. Simple."

Shielka threw her head back and looked defiantly at Talos and said, "Yes, we must kill them. I, Shielka, last Seer of the Ikano, swear that I will have vengeance upon those that slaughtered my people. They will perish as my people perished, totally and without mercy. Talos, you must accept their offer to meet with their Queen."

Shielka's eyes were focused upon Talos and energy began to crackle in the air around her.

"Yes. Yes, of course I'll accept. Just stay calm Shielka. We will help you avenge your peoples' deaths but first we must have a plan. Just relax and sit down and let's discuss how best to proceed."

Ceylon spoke, "Yes, we must have a plan. Their Queen is surely going to have guards around her and we must be prepared for them. Shielka, you have great powers but still cannot control them fully. You have mastered the Orb and it will let you command it, but what will you command it to do?"

Shielka turned away from them and took several deep breaths.

Turning back to face them again she said, "I will command it to do what needs to be done."

They made their plans.

After a while the sun began its slow assent into the morning sky, Ceylon spotted the two Demons flying toward them.

"They are coming."

Talos turned toward Shielka and said, "Remember the plan and be alert, but please stay calm."

Shielka tilted her head forward and looked down at the ground and nodded. Her left hand was cupped around the bottom of the small pouch that hung at her waist. Her right hand was resting on the hilt of her long jeweled dagger.

"Shielka quit playing with the Orb. We must not let the Demons discover it," whispered Talos.

Shielka pulled her hand away from the pouch and walked toward the remnants of their camp fire.

Talos watched her walk away and was about to call to her again when Ceylon said, "They are here."

Zak and Arnot landed together on the same spot that Zak had occupied the night before.

Zak asked, "What is your answer?"

"We will visit your Queen to discuss her share of my world," said Talos.

"Our world," said Ceylon.

A sneer formed on Talos's face as he sarcastically said to Ceylon, "Yes, of course... Our world."

Zak watched and listened intently as the two Elves parried with words.

"Do all of you have the ability to fly?" asked Zak.

"Ceylon and I will assist the girl."

"Come, let us go," said Zak.

Zak and Arnot spread their wings and took off into the morning sky.

Ceylon cast a spell upon himself to allow him to fly magically.

Talos pulled a black cloak out of his pack and put it on. He then said, "Wings" and the cloak grew into an enormous pair of bat wings that grafted themselves into Talos's back. He extended the wings and gently flew off of the ground.

Shielka reached out and took hold of Ceylon's hand and then she was lifted off on the ground and they began flying toward the coast.

Zak and Arnot were in the lead and the others followed behind them.

Zak turned to Arnot and said, "Did you hear them speak to each other? We will wait to kill them. We may be able to use their petty grievances against each other to our advantage."

Arnot said, "We should kill them."

Zak looked back at Talos, Ceylon and the girl.

"Why does the girl look so familiar?" he said aloud to himself.

Arnot responded, "She is from the islands."

Zak turned and faced Arnot while still maintaining his forward flight and said, "What?"

"She wears the mark of the Ikano. She is of Maraka's tribe."

"But all on that island were killed."

Then he looked back at those following him and studied the girl more intently. For the first time he noticed her clothing. She was wearing a heavy cloak that covered her from head to toe. The night before she was different.

"What was she wearing before?"

Talos was watching Zak's behavior and flew closer to Ceylon and said, "I'm worried. I think he's figured out where Shielka is from. He keeps looking back here at her."

"Perhaps. Perhaps not. But we must be very careful. Are you alright Shielka?"

Shielka had never flown before and the feeling was strange. The sights she could see were incredible. She didn't know if she should be happy or sick.

She held closely to Ceylon and replied, "I'm fine. I just wish that the Demon would quit looking back at me."

"Be careful what you wish for Shielka, it may come true in ways you don't expect. Never throw wishes around casually."

Shielka had a puzzled look on her face. She didn't know if Ceylon was kidding or being serious so she just said, "I'll be careful."

They flew for a long time without speaking.

Eventually Talos broke the silence by calling up to Zak, "Zak, it is afternoon now. We must rest. My wings grow tired and Ceylon's spell is near its completion."

Zak waved and began a gradual descent to the ground.

He picked a barren outcropping of rock and dirt along the bank of a narrow river on which to land.

"Rest here. We will be back at sunset to begin again."

Then Zak and Arnot took off.

Talos said to Ceylon and Shielka, "We must eat and get some sleep. This is going to be a long journey in a short time."

"I will try and catch some fish. Shielka, you can gather some wood for the fire," said Ceylon.

"I will not."

Talos and Ceylon looked at her blankly and Ceylon said, "What?"

"I will not gather wood while you try and catch fish. I was raised from birth surrounded by fishermen. My Seer training allowed me to call to the fish and make bountiful harvests from the sea. Why should I gather wood while you relax catching fish?"

"Well... I just thought that... I mean... OK, you catch the fish and I'll gather the wood."

Talos laughed quietly to himself.

Shielka turned to face Talos and said, "What are you laughing at. Go and help Ceylon gather wood, we haven't got all day you know."

Talos stepped back from Shielka and sheepishly replied, "OK."

Ceylon and Talos walked toward the trees shaking their heads.

Shielka watched them leave and then she sat down and looked into the water. She sent her mind forth and felt the tingling sensation of contact with many fish. She smiled to herself knowing that she could have as many as she wanted. Looking into the water she saw her reflection and was shocked by what she saw.

Her long red hair was knotted and matted against her head and tear stains streaked down her cheeks.

"Oh, those two idiots. How could they let me walk around looking like this and not say anything?"

Shielka lay down on the shore and lowered her head into the water. The water was cool and refreshing. She pulled her head out of the water and began washing her face and trying to untangle her hair. She put her head into the water again to rinse it out.

Suddenly a heavy weight fell down upon her back and a hand slammed into the back of her head, holding her head under the water.

Shielka tried to move but the weight was too heavy and the hand too strong.

"I'm drowning," she thought, "I'm drowning..."

CHAPTER 26: THE STAFF

Aka'r watched in horror as the huge Demon flew up to catch the staff. The Demon was only seconds from reaching the Staff and Aka'r stretched out his hand and said, "Lightning!"

Instantly a streak of light shot from his pointing hand and formed itself into a long Lightning Bolt. The bolt flew through the air and struck the Demon just as his long claws were closing around the shaft of the Staff.

The Demon was knocked slightly to one side and its clawed hands grasped empty air instead of the staff. It turned its horrible head and faced Aka'r and Fal'r. Then it looked down at the falling staff and began a quick dive toward the ground.

Aka'r pointed at the path in front of the Demon and said, "Fireball!"

A pea sized object shot from his hand and streaked toward the Demon's path. The small object mushroomed rapidly and grew in size as it traveled.

While Aka'r was casting his spell, Fal'r was busy casting a spell of his own. Fal'r reached out his hand and pointing toward the staff and said, "Ice Shield!"

A shimmering glow appeared a few feet above the staff and grew into an icy sphere that encompassed it, the ice caked staff continued to fall.

The Demon flew toward the Staff and encountered the Ice barrier. It bellowed its frustration and rage in a deep guttural howl. Simultaneously the Fireball sent by Aka'r slammed into the Demon and the Ice Shield. A great cloud of fog was created by the intense heat of the Fireball rapidly melting the Ice Shield. The fog cloud completely obscured the Demon and the Staff from Fal'r and Aka'rs' view.

Sure Shot pulled out his magic bow and was about to fire at the Demon when the Fireball hit the Ice Shield.

He said to Iron Fist, "What do I do now? I can't see them."

"Don't shoot. We can't risk hitting Aka'r."

Iron fist then began running at full speed toward where the Staff and Demon should be hitting the ground.

Sure Shot stayed where he was with his bow in hand. He kept a watchful eye on the fog cloud waiting for it to clear. He yearned to let his magic arrows fly into the horrible Demon.

Sparrow watched all that had occurred and was transfixed by the powers she had seen unleashed against the Demon.

She said to Spike, "I must go into the fog and help them against the Demon, you wait here."

She turned and stepped into an evergreen tree and vanished from Spike's sight.

Spike did not understand what was going on but was not content to wait. He was curious to see where his new friend was going so he began an easy trot toward the fog.

Andromeda and Tama'r had lost sight of the others and Tama'r had cast her spell of Farseeing to scout around the area to try and find them. She saw a woman dressed all in green step behind a tree but not appear on the other side. She sent her magic eye around the tree and Tama'r was amazed to see no trace of her. She looked down at the ground and saw footprints that led directly into tree. Tama'r looked around the area and spotted a Unicorn Rabbit running between the trees. Instinctively she caused her magic eye to follow the rabbit. The rabbit wasn't moving very quickly but it was running in a straight line.

Tama'r decided to move her eye ahead of it and see where it was going.

Looking ahead of the rabbit Tama'r saw the unnatural fog cloud and Aka'r and Fal'r flying toward it. Tama'r noticed immediately that Fal'r no longer had the Staff and she abruptly ended the spell.

She turned to face Andromeda and said, "We must run, quickly, Fal'r has lost the staff in a huge fog cloud. Something is very wrong."

Andromeda's mouth fell open and she nodded in a stunned silence. They both quickly began running. Tama'r was in the lead as she knew which path to take.

Tama'r did not turn to speak with her companion. She just raised her right arm and waved over her shoulder. She disappeared from Andromeda's view around one of the many turns in the path. Andromeda kept running at her own steady pace.

The Demon could not see in the heavy fog that surrounded him. But he felt the power of the Staff and it called to his very essence. He felt the raw power emanating from it. It guided him like a signal fire in the night, down, into the trees and brush. The trees here were thick, but not so thick that he couldn't crush and bend them with his mighty strength. He began making his way slowly toward the staff.

Fal'r cast another Flying spell on himself and both he and Aka'r hovered above the Fog Cloud.

Aka'r said, "Why did you cast an Ice Shield of all things?"

"Me? At least I know that Demons live and breath fire and flames. So you cast a Fireball?"

Aka'r shrugged.

Fal'r continued, "At least an Ice Shield is foreign to him and would have provided some protection. Don't you know any Control Weather or Wind spells that we can use?"

"If I had any readied don't you think I would have used one?"

"Why can't we just shoot into the fog and hope for the best?"

"We can't afford to use up our spells when we don't know if they'll do any good."

While Aka'r and Fal'r were discussing what to do next Sparrow stepped out of a tree and into the dense fog. She looked around but could see nothing. Even the tree behind her was a blur. Only a small bit of light was filtering down to her and the trees and bushes took on ominous dark forms. Sparrow withdrew her sword from its sheath and held it tightly in her hand, and listened.

She heard the trees scream as their limbs were torn from them. Then she heard the heavy footfalls of the Demon approaching. She wanted to weep for the poor plants but furious rage was building up inside of her. She heard the Demon coming closer and she tried to move behind the tree, but she tripped on a root and fell crashing to the ground. The back of her hand crashed down upon a rock and her sword went flying from her hand. It fell away into the misty darkness of the fog.

The Demon was almost to the Staff and he could feel its closeness. The intensity of the Staff's power was euphoric. Then the Demon stopped moving. One of the puny humans was there, he could smell it.

"Kill human," he thought.

But the gigantic Demon continued on toward the pulsating power of the Staff.

Iron Fist was standing at the base of the fog cloud when Tama'r came running up to him.

"Iron Fist, what happened? I saw Sure Shot but he didn't say anything."

"A Demon is within the fog and is searching for the staff. Aka'r and Fal'r are above the cloud but have not entered. It is too thick even for us to enter. So we wait for it to go."

"Why doesn't Aka'r or Fal'r dispel the cloud?"

"I do not know."

Tama'r raised her hands, high above her head, and gave the command, "Wind!"

A small breeze started to blow by her. Then a gust and then a strong wind. It gradually began dissipating the Fog.

"Very good Tama'r. Keep it up, stronger now."

"Look Aka'r, the fog cloud is breaking up, it's Tama'r. Good work Tama'r", yelled Fal'r.

"But now the Demon can see as well. We must find the Staff before it does."

Aka'r began a slow descent into the thinning fog.

Sparrow heard the Demon crashing through the trees coming directly toward her. She saw the Fog starting to clear and began to stand up. Pain shot up through her leg from her ankle and she fell back to the ground. A deep sharp and throbbing pain in her ankle told her it was broken. The Demon was getting closer and she groped for her sword. She couldn't find it.

As the fog cleared she saw the massive form of the Demon getting closer. She called upon the trees to help her and they spread their branches into the Demons path. But the Demon just ripped them apart and kept coming toward her.

The Demon saw the human girl and his prize. He grinned a wide grin in a mouth full of sharp, pointed teeth. In two strides he would have his prize.

Spike came hopping through the trees and ran up behind the Demon. Spike wanting to protect his friend gave a mighty hop and speared the Demon in the behind with his sharp, foot long, horn.

The Demon howled in pain as he spun around to fight this pest. The Demon was faster than Spike realized and Spike was unable to jump away quickly enough to avoid the Demons claws.

The Demon reached out one of its huge clawed hands and grabbed Spike around the neck. Sparrow heard a snapping sound and she saw Spike fall from the Demons grasp. Spikes limp body hit the ground with a dull thud.

Sparrow screamed and looked around for a weapon.

"A cudgel," she thought.

Looking down at where her foot hung lifeless at the end of her leg, Sparrow found the root she had tripped on. Then she noticed the carvings on it and gasped.

Quickly she reached for the Staff and as her fingers closed they gripped tightly around the hot rough surface of the Demon's massive claw. The Demon had grabbed the Staff first. Sparrow's screams could be heard for miles.

www.ingramcontent.com/pod-product-compliance
Lightning Source LLC
Chambersburg PA
CBHW071256130626
46556CB00003B/1342